T0128810

KNOWING

ME

KNOWING ME

JASMINE FLEUR

KNOWING ME

This is a work of fiction. All of the characters, names, incidents, organizations, and dialogue in this novel are either the products of the author's imagination or are used fictitiously.

iUniverse books may be ordered through booksellers or by contacting:

iUniverse
1663 Liberty Drive
Bloomington, IN 47403
www.iuniverse.com
1-800-Authors (1-800-288-4677)

Because of the dynamic nature of the Internet, any web addresses or links contained in this book may have changed since publication and may no longer be valid. The views expressed in this work are solely those of the author and do not necessarily reflect the views of the publisher, and the publisher hereby disclaims any responsibility for them.

Any people depicted in stock imagery provided by Thinkstock are models, and such images are being used for illustrative purposes only. Certain stock imagery © Thinkstock.

ISBN: 978-1-5320-0514-5 (sc)
ISBN: 978-1-5320-0517-6 (e)

Library of Congress Control Number: 2016913822

Print information available on the last page.

iUniverse rev. date: 09/28/2016

CHAPTER 1

INTRODUCTION INTO MY WORLD

It all started when I was a little girl. I thought that playing in an alternate world was better than playing with children in the neighbourhood. The games best played were the ones that took my mind off the perpetual arguments and lack of food in my house. I would play a lot of games, and these made my imagination wander. The games took me elsewhere, with role playing and scenarios. Most of the time, I pretended I was a cook or someone who had a store and could sell items to make money. I imagined being rich and played games with my imaginary friends and dolls. I also played games that made me think of fairy tale characters in stories like *Cinderella*. I would think of better things that put me in a better place.

I sit trying to gather my memories, thinking as far back as I can, but I think my best memories are from about ten years old. I must have blocked many earlier memories; my mind may have been too fanciful to retain information prior to that, or I was too young to understand. I also know that I tried to block all the nastiness I experienced because it was easier to keep good memories than bad.

God knows my parents tried, but it was always a struggle to feed three children and two adults. Mom was a hard worker and tried to tie all loose ends. My dad tried too; however, he was a dreamer and dreamt beyond his reach. My dad was not healthy and suffered from heart problems and other issues. My mom was really strong and a fighter, but she was not educated and was ill equipped to get a great job. God, how I love this woman, and I owe her so much. She is amazing, and I will never try to paint her in a negative light. She did whatever she could to make her little girl as happy as could be. I try to think that my life was not that bad, but it was really tough. You will come to your own conclusions as you travel with me.

Then again, who am I to complain? Look at all the starving children around the world, and look at all the human trafficking. It's something for us all to think about as we go along our dour lives. This rambling may be confusing, but hopefully it will be clearer as you get to know me. I am not amazing, and neither am I trying to prove I'm better than anyone else. However, I do think that each of us, no matter how good or bad we are deemed by society, can be cognizant of the things we can positively affect. It takes only a few minutes to make an effort and add to a gigantic momentum of events. As I tell my story, I hope you find some relevance to your life or other events that you can control.

I love my parents so much and wished I could do something to help and make money magically appear; then they would be rich with no worries. Even at ten years old, I did not care about material things for myself. I simply wanted everyone to be happy and have no more arguments. Desperate times meant desperate people at their wits' ends. This made it easier for my parents to deal with their lives, by reacting in anger and lashing out at each other. Money seemed to be the solution to all our needs, but looking back, was it really money, or being stuck in a situation where my dad never got to know or experience his full potential? I know that we needed the money, but if we had tried to make do with what we had and tried harder to get by, it may not have been as bad as dreaming and wishing for miracles.

I figure my father tried to be a good parent by sharing his mind, reading a lot, and imparting his knowledge as much as he could. He read aloud, and even if we didn't want to listen, the words stuck in our minds. Because I was the girl in the family and was never allowed to play too much with other children, I became the one stuck indoors, and I was stuck with the words implanted in my mind even now. I could not run away from his voice! The home was tiny and was made up of rooms and corners that carried sounds like in a box. I never thought my home was small; I was simply happy to have a place in which to be safe.

My father spent a lot of time reading and thinking of future plans, but maybe he could have spent more time focusing on the here and now. I was not in his shoes; how would I know what he did best to cope with his life? I do know that it is hard to survive and provide for a family, even in the best of situations, and we were in the lower half.

My father was always thinking big, but I think he was frustrated with not being able to act on his dreams. He had grandiose ideas of wealth, a huge house, and unlimited luxuries. He made us believe that these dreams would materialise. He would tell us of his future world and reel us in, giving us false hope. He was intelligent academically, but he was not so smart when it came to planning real-life situations. He dragged us into his mindset, which made each failed dream so much worse to accept. We became fixated on these things happening, and we never questioned him. We thought that these dreams would come true.

My family was pretty traditional and old-fashioned. My dad's expectations were for me to be conservative and kept in control – meaning no dating, no fun, and no life experiences. He thought girls should not go out into the world on their own; they should get a job, get married, have children, and be safe. He was too rigid with my upbringing and wanted to control all of his children. His method of parenting was to place a fear of his wrath in our minds. He wanted respect, but we all know that respect is earned, not demanded; you will only get fear, and in time fear is replaced by resentment.

I know what most of you may be thinking: he was a bad dad. But on the contrary, I think most of his thought process was due to ignorance. His anger was mostly driven by a lack of money, but intrinsically I believe the lost dreams played a part in my father's frustrations. He meant well, but his parenting skills needed a lot of work.

When he read all his books, all his words somehow stayed in my mind. Even though all the books he read with big words seemed such a headache in my childhood, subconsciously I must have known that he was smart and that these words would somehow make a difference in my train of thought and my future. I started looking at the books my dad read, and when I was alone, I would pick up these books. I was alone quite often because my brothers were always with their friends, and my parents would be somewhere trying to earn money – doing what, I was not quite sure. I never quite thought much of it; my life for the most part was oblivious acceptance. I guess I got peace of mind out of making my life seem normal, and the less I knew, the better.

In retrospect, most likely they were out hustling to get money through whatever means. My parents sold the fruits from our yard; they would take large baskets laden with fruits to the market in the wee hours of the mornings in order to get their goods sold early in the day. They also tried selling my mother's sewing of children's clothes to a few vendors; it was a much harder sale because the vendors were tardy on their payments. My parents tried as much as they could to provide for us. I have tried to analyse what could be done differently, but the truth is they gave all their energies and hopes into daily sustenance, and I am grateful for the little treats my mom would sneak for me. My mom wanted me to have pretty things and sweets, so when she could put together a little cash, she would secretively give me these little surprises. Bless my mother's heart!

When I was alone, I hunted through my dad's books, and I would read lots. I read *Othello, Great Expectations, Sons and Lovers,* and *Chapters of Life.* I found that because these books were written in a different era, it made my imagination soak up every bit of character and story. Thus bloomed my love for reading. I was a very late reader, and my parents thought I was not so smart, until at the age of five when I picked up a book written by Enid Blyton named *Mr. Pink-Whistle.* Since then, I could not stop reading. My dad had tried so hard, and sometimes I think he thought I was slow and unable to understand anything. He was a teacher, and once I was literate, he was so happy that I got books for every occasion, when he could afford it.

It's surreal how the world seems a better place when one's immersed in a good book, because it offers that escape. Such becomes the lives of many people (including myself) who feel the need to go into an imaginary state when reality slaps them on the cheek too often.

The reality of my life was too much for my innocent mind, and the best escape was through imagination. I think many of us poor people end up in meaningless relationships or submit to other vices. Sometimes we try to escape by other means. I tried my way, and this was how I did it. When I was a few years older, I imagined an alternate life with my few toys, choosing to play under the desk, barring the entrance by placing cardboard at it, and pretending that my two dolls were eating the best foods. It made me feel that I had friends and was part of that world where good and delicious foods were free. I played these games when we had moved to another place to live, and I did not have my dad's books to read because they were thrown away or lost. I didn't have my reading world.

I would be left home alone and would get hungry, but I'd not have any food to eat. I think my parents forgot that this little girl was left home alone with a totally scared mind, and I wouldn't try to move from my spot under the desk. Sometimes hunger pangs bit me harshly, making it unbearable for me to play, but I had to play to make it through the day, until my mom would come back home with maybe something to eat. Simply having her home made it more bearable. If you have ever experienced true hunger, you will understand. I was not suffering from malnutrition (at least, I didn't think so), and I got something to eat each day, but I did not get three meals daily. Hours and days and years went by without much significance, because the need to be fed was paramount. The need to be normal and accepted was right up there with my top priorities. My life as a child had very clear memories, but some were a long blur with images affixed in my mind. Such was my life for a few years: perpetual hunger and being left alone at home, with no friends and being too scared to leave home to go for walks or have fun.

For hours and hours, I would stay under the desk. When my brother Brad was home, he would taunt me and call me names. He thought I was weird, and this made me feel I was not safe from the ugliness that existed beyond the cardboard walls. I knew that he was mean, but sometimes I think he saw that I was troubled, and he wanted to help me in the only way he knew. Brad also thought I was stupid, and he wanted me to stop being such a baby and grow up. He only saw a grown girl under a desk playing with dolls by herself. He never knew what went on in my mind and only saw this pitiful older girl refusing to grow up and being socially unacceptable.

Brad was someone I could have been closer with in those years, but we were so different that I think we lived in different realms. Sadly, he became much more troubled than I would ever be. My parents were too busy to be concerned with his whereabouts; again, those of you who grew up like me will understand. Parents who are poor are more concerned about putting food on the table and trying to survive each day, without having someone banging on their door for bills. My parents did spend some time with us, and we went to the movies as a treat, but my brothers refused to go with us. My brothers didn't want to be seen with my parents because they were ashamed of them. We went to movies my parents wanted to see. Brad became a low priority on the list. Also, he was never around, so even if my parents had a few moments where they could have spent with him, he wasn't there.

My brothers preferred to hang out with their friends because they had more fun. Whenever they were with my parents, they were disciplined. I was treated much better because I really did not get the opportunity to do any wrong. I guess if I had the same treatment and freedom my brothers had, I would have done exactly the same as they did. I also did not like giving my parents a hard time, so I figured it was easier to stay out of trouble.

I had a few friends at school, but they were very different from me. They had so much money and things, and they were pretty, clean, and well dressed. They always had so much food at lunchtime and even snacks to eat during the day. I would look at them hungrily, hoping they would share, but this hardly ever happened. I came to see, even at a young age, that being rich does not mean that everyone shares; rather, people like keep to themselves or throw away their extras. At least, that is what I thought happened at this time of my life. It seemed as if rich people lived in a different world; theirs was a world of privileges and luxuries I would only come to know in my later years. I became resentful and found it hard to be friends with these children. It's always good to look back and see how much we can change our opinions of what happened in our past.

I remembered sitting in the classroom at the new school which my dad insisted I attend. As a teacher, he wanted the best for me, and he hoped by some miracle all his children would prosper and grow into successful adults. He went through a lot of humiliation to get me accepted to this school. He had to beg the headmistress of the school, and I am sure he had to humiliate himself for my acceptance. This was a privileged institution, meaning it was only for the rich and influential. This was something I always will remember and appreciate, even when he was mean to my mom and I hated him for the way he treated her. He tried his best to get me an education, but he could not support me to pursue my dreams later in life; we simply couldn't afford it. At least he gave me the tools to be prepared and figure out my way.

Every time I have a flashback and remember him treating my mom badly, I try to make excuses for him. I would say because he was hung up on some older traditions, where men were the head of the household and were supposed to be in charge as the bread winner, he could not fulfil his perceived role, and so he reacted in the way he did. I also try to think of him not being able to provide for his family and being frustrated and sad. To him, women were not equal, especially my mom; I think this was because of the way he was condescending towards my mom all the time. It made me sick, and it still does. I knew later it was not all women – he simply wanted to control my mom, and he did this through fear and intimidation. I think he was disappointed in himself but needed to blame someone, and if he made my mom feel smaller than him, then she would look up to him. Sadly, this was my mother's life. This approach let him feel some amount of power and control in his life.

Man, he was really mean to my mom. I never knew just how my mom took it, but took it she did. We were definitely not a touchy-feely family; I have no memories of any of us hugging each other or declaring words of love and affection. My mom's heart must have been broken into a thousand pieces during her lifetime. There was no closeness with any of us towards each other. If there had been an opening for hugs and kisses, I think we all could have been closer. We could have figured out a way of being better people, together.

Because of this, none of the children ever felt good about talking or going to my parents for consolation. We did not feel the connection and knew that we would be adding to their stress. I did not know this was not normal; I simply knew that whenever I cried, it seemed like I had to figure out why I was sad by myself. That sounds really weird, but it was not really, just terribly confusing to someone so young. I always felt confused and somewhat misplaced, and I always thought almost everyone was better than me. All of these things happening in my life contributed towards my lack of social skills, which were clearly nonexistent. It will always be a hurdle to try to appear normal, with societal normalcy being what it is. I am still challenged to blend in amongst people most of the times, but I surmount that fear.

My poor mom had her own torments and worked into the wee hours of the morning. She never complained and just plugged away on her sewing machine, day in and day out without electricity, using a manual foot handle to pump the machine. She sewed clothes and met buyers' deadlines to put food on the table. The sad thing is all that work, pain, and long-term suffering tallied to just a small percentage of profit, which basically went into groceries. I will always have that mental picture of my mom, her head bowed and shoulders slumped in the dimly lit room, pressing her feet down rhythmically trying to sew children's clothing. And I'll always shy away from hunger and poverty with fear, drenched with worry over the possibility. It shall be a constant battle for me to be better, for me to accomplish more and try to not be in need or to have my children suffer the same fate. This is my life promise and challenge.

My dad, bless his intentions, bought all the storybooks from the bookstore in the city. That money could have most likely put more food on the table or given us new clothes, but for my dad, education was the priority even if we had to eat one loaf of bread with sugar and water. I remember going to bed hungry, but I never complained and kept all my thoughts to myself. I passed my afternoons after school indoors reading and sometimes drawing. I seemed to be good at drawing sketches and doodling. I also did quite a bit of people watching, although I am sure now that all my people watching went detected; man, I must have been seen as some wacko child. I chuckle at this because it is quite funny, and hopefully I will never encounter these people again! I became obsessed with people and would sit at the window for hours, watching as people went by. Sometimes I would sit on a bench in the yard, with the sun lighting my face and thoughts. I'd look at passersby and imagine who they really were and what they were thinking.

I often wondered how my friends passed their afternoons. I would hear them talking about events and things at school, of friends visiting their homes and going to private lessons, hobbies, and birthday parties. I wanted to know how I got to be a part of that world. They would talk about meeting after school, sleeping over, and hanging out. It sounded so strange to me. At home, I would see the neighbourhood children gathering and running off to play games, laughter following them, and I sat in the same spot until they ran past again. As I grew, I got the distinct impression – as a matter of fact, I was told – that everyone thought I was a snotty child who would not deign to play with the other kids. So much for the truth, eh? It was because of my visual projection: I was always clean and dressed well, even with so few pieces of clothing, and I carried myself with pride.

Imagine that: I was the poorest of the lot and could not think of playing with the others, because I did not want them to know anything about me. I was afraid that once they knew how poor I was, once they learned about my life and my family, they would make fun of me. I would have given anything during my childhood to be one of these children running around in the streets and having carefree fun!

I had no clue about my life beyond getting dressed every school day, eating whatever was given to me eagerly and thankfully, sometimes bathing if there was soap and water, powdering my armpits to prevent any odours, dressing neatly, and always taking care to look presentable. Then I focused on either walking to school with my mom or by myself. And this was my life for quite a few years, and it was fine with me because once I got to school, my days flew by. I did not realize I was above average in intelligence. I got engrossed in my schoolwork, and it seemed easy and natural to understand. It also seemed natural to get almost perfect scores; I did not realize it put me on the radar for bullying and targeting by others. For me, this was part of making the days go by without having to think about all the real things in my life.

There were two boys who thought it was fun to make fun of me. They always tried to take away my desk, move my chair, or pull my hair. I never did much in retaliation, but I survived by introspecting. It was hard for me to stand up for myself because I never quite fit in at school with all these rich children and pretty things. I did have an assertive way of looking at people, though I was not aware of it, and this saved me when words failed me. I am guessing it's the survival instinct we all have, and if we're accustomed to tough situations, we develop that protective shell. I would put on a scary expression in the hopes of scaring them away, but I think they stopped because they did not have much fun as much as in the beginning, and it was too much work for them to bother me. I do wish my childhood had more fun and light in my memories; it is difficult to go down memory lane.

Things would change – for better or worse, you can come to your own thinking. It all depends on how we look at my life. As it turn out, my life was quite an adventure, and I will share some of my experiences with you.

CHAPTER 2

My Brothers

Brad was two years older than me, and even though he sometimes teased me, in his mind it was for my own good. Even though we were not close when we were younger, and I thought he was very mean to me, I found out later that he was only trying in his way to help me to be normal and happy. As we got older, we became very close, and I loved him very much. My older brother Anthony was totally different and not close to either of his siblings; he was eight years older than me and was always hanging out with his friends. My parents were so busy trying to make ends meet that no one paid much attention to any of us. This was a shame because Anthony had a lot of potential, and so did Brad. I think because I was the girl and the youngest, I got most of my parents' attention; also, I was the only one ever at home. I do believe because my brothers felt ignored and unloved, these feelings, along with choices, may have also led to my brothers' demise. I was too fearful of the unknown to tread in the paths my brothers took; I did not question what my parents taught me. I think I suffered from non-participation in living, if there is such an illness or categorization.

My older brother was handsome, tall, and athletic. His friends were even better looking and intimidating, so I always stayed clear of them, feeling somewhat invisible and inferior. These were teenagers who seemed cool and out of touch. As time went by, it became clear to me that it was a good thing I stayed clear because all of his friends were drug takers; they smoked pot, and this made my brother tumble into the dark path for the rest of his life. He would never come out of this hole and would become a lifelong drug addict.

He was always hanging out with his friends, and because our dad was old-fashioned, he thought that boys should be boys and could go anywhere and stay out as long as they wanted to, with no supervision. Anthony therefore had no guidance or fear of restrictions. He thought he had the world to conquer and would do it his way. He did fear my dad, but he was never around to be chastised, and my parents were constantly tired and had no energy to focus on him. He knew that he could get away with all that he did.

His friends were all wealthy and were used to getting anything they wanted. Anthony started using drugs, and no one checked on him. Never was he told he should not do it, and no one asked him where he went and what he did until it was too late.

Anthony would sleep over with his friends, or they would break into a school during the weekend and have a cookout with stolen food items, stealing a chicken from a neighbour's coop and partying throughout the night. My brother was so handsome and popular. He won many races (when he participated in school sports events) and was an excellent runner. Then eventually his interest wandered, and he stopped running.

I have to mention more on my brothers so you can understand what happened in my world, not just to me but to those closest to me. Just when I thought that in my younger years life was as bad as it could ever be, things took an even darker and sadder twist that made me question life.

CHAPTER 3

DETRIMENTAL AND DOMINO EVENTS

The first time my dad became ill was a blurry time in my life, but I remember bits and pieces. I remember waking up, and the place was dark, dank, and dirty. That was not unusual from every other day, but it was even darker and had a sense of foreboding, an almost evil feeling. I recall my mom steering me clear of my parents' bedroom, but I also remember seeing my dad looking scarily thin and smelling. My dad never smelled. I remember rats scurrying under his bed and shadows flitting in his room – or was it my imagination? I remember that my mom seemed sad and frail and was too busy to even look at me. I do not remember anything else clearly, but I knew that I did not see my dad for several days. I was not allowed to go near his bed, and as a scared little child, I did what I was told.

I remember blurred moments. I think months passed. If you are a child who is scared and left alone to deal with thoughts and feelings, time can go by really fast, or days can appear to be weeks. It's called living in a surreal world, coping with just enough to survive. I do not remember eating, playing, or reading. I only remember coming home from school one day long after and seeing my dad weakly sitting in a chair. I was so happy but was not allowed near him. I think my mom was trying to keep me from being scared in her own way. Or my dad was still too sick to be pestered by a little girl who wanted to know everything.

This was one event that would stay in my mind as truly traumatic. I have never spoken about this to anyone. It is something that one suppresses in details and skims over; it was a scary moment. Days passed, my dad recovered, and all seemed normal. I was breathing easy and felt alive again, and I started reading. At this stage, I had started borrowing books from my friends – and I borrowed a lot!

My dad seemed okay, but things started to slowly change. Anthony had to start working to help out at home. He was not happy but was told he had to, or we would not have enough to eat. My poor brother never stood a chance against the blows that life and my dad dealt to him. I make no excuses for his mistakes; rather, I try to explain the path he would take. I recall my brother coming home one day with blood running down his legs. He had been bitten by a dog. He had a job as a delivery boy for a local post office and had dropped out of school at the age of fourteen. I felt so sorry for him, but again, I did not know why until much later. I know I appear to be quite obtuse and stupid. I will make no excuses. I did not realize just how much I loved my brothers and cared for my family – the mistakes, the problems, the sadness, all of it. Imagine your life as a teenager, running amok one moment and the next being responsible for bringing food to the family table. And still you are not getting any love or support as you flounder.

My dad was too sick and had to leave his teaching job of more than eighteen years. My mom was sewing and selling clothes as our only source of income, and my parents seemed so totally separated, each with a part to play in the game of survival. Things became even tougher.

I could not remember ever really being hugged, and I know I said we were not a touchy-feely family, but children do crave that feeling to be hugged. I am not blaming anyone because my parents were so busy, and emotions were never really considered. However, my mom would try to buy me little things to make me happy – things like hairpins, ribbons, and even socks. My mom became worn out in these years, with age catching up so quickly, and her looks deteriorated, but not her inner strength. How I love my mom. She was so beautiful and quiet, and she never complained about anything in her life. She always tried to make sure I ate when she was home, even if she had no food for herself.

When my dad got sick for the first time, I saw in my mom display so much strength. I never really worried too much about my dad being ill, because my mom tried to make it seem normal, with no visible changes to a ten-year-old living sometimes in a dream world to escape from reality.

My mom knew I liked making things, so she bought me beads. Beads were really cheap, so I did not feel guilty about her taking money to get me these. I would take the beads my mom bought for me and make little clothes for my dolls. I was creative at a very young age, emulating my mom's sewing. Sometimes I'd prick myself with the needles, but I went on, never quitting. I used the beads to make awesome designs on the dresses. This made me happy when the little dresses looked so pretty, and I felt like I'd accomplished something and could do what my mom did. I also learnt the sense of never quitting but focusing on any task or life-changing decision in my life.

My mom would tell me how pretty the dresses were, and how I could do anything I wanted because I was so smart.

I wasn't old enough to bear the responsibilities, and I wasn't made to suffer through the harsh realities my two brothers had to go through. I recall my older brother dropping out of school, and my smaller brother hanging out with even richer children. Brad was left alone also, and he eventually made the same mistakes as Anthony; his life took a turn for the worse. He would spend weekends with his friends. I believe Brad did not know how to accept his circumstances, which was why he hung out with rich people and was so ashamed of his life; he had been unhappy since he was old enough to understand. I miss him terribly. I miss the chance to have spent time with him, to let him know it was okay and that I would always be there for him. I am so sorry that I never got to tell him that I love him. Sometimes when those we love leave this world, we have so many regrets. Even if we are cognizant and try to be loving at all times, there are always things we wish we'd said or done.

As Brad started hanging out with older friends, his attitude became angry and belligerent. He would bring home groceries from the store of his friend Bandido. Bandido was an older guy who seemed very strange, even to me, but my parents would behave as if nothing was wrong when there obviously was. It came to an end one day when my mom could not take it anymore and told his friend off. I sometimes wondered what happened, and then my imagination would get the better of me, and I would be sickened. My poor brother was such a nice boy before "real life" happened to him. He had such promise, such brightness; my grandmother saw that in him. I hope that my brother did not have to go through what my imagination assumes.

Brad fluctuated between extreme quiet and extreme anger. I loved him and always wanted to hang out with him, having no real friends of my own, but sometimes his friends would laugh at me or try hitting me, so I eventually gave up out of fear of being hurt. I never told him because I did not want him to be angry with his friends and fight and get hurt.

When he got older, he made several attempts to be closer to me, and I did become closer to him. At this stage I was quite separated from my family, and shame and sadness seemed to be the theme of my life. I evaded them and even looked away several times when passing them on the streets, hoping that they would not see me. What a terrible thing to do. However, I made amends for these acts and tried as best as I could to make up for time lost and love not given. My memories will not let me. Those of you who have done similar things know how hard it is to accept it. We were once so cold and stupid! I am so sad when I travel the path of nostalgia, and I remember how stupid I was and the people I took for granted. To some people I gave too much, when they did not deserve anything from me.

I became someone with dreams; here, I became like my dad. I had a great imagination and decided this provided the ultimate escape from reality. Being a little child did not make me immune to all that was happening around me. I dreamt of growing up and being far away from my life; I imagined a world with no fear or shame, and with lots to eat and really nice clothes. In my world, I had lots of friends and was the pretty girl, and all the kids wanted to be around me. I imagined talking about parties and sleepovers and fancy dishes and clothes and shows.

I thought of so many ways to become famous and rich, and I spent most of my time day dreaming. It seemed to make me feel better until hunger bit into my stomach, or I was invited to a real party and was unable to make it. My parents did not have enough money for a gift or money for a new dress, and my dad did not want me to be corrupted. I think my dad saw that my brothers were already lost, and his only hope was to make me successful and do good things with my life. I really wish they had allowed me to be a child and let me go to parties and fairs, doing fun things with friends. My dad was good; however, he thought if he let me go out or have friends, "bad things" would happen to me. I was stuck at home with dismal feelings floating in the air. How nice it would have been to go play with my friends.

Looking back at my childhood, I knew that all was not as bad as it appeared. This is not a dismal story, but merely a rendition of my life at that time. My parents loved me a lot, and in the time and things they spent and did with me, when we could, I know they'd never let any harm befall me. I am grateful for all that they have done, and I think of parents who have so much more to offer yet never think it is part of their live acts. Life is short, so give as much as you can. It makes you feel so good and as if the world is much smaller, where you can see all angles and planes.

I have good memories too. I would have peaceful moments where everything seemed just right. I can think back to days like this. The birds were always chirping on the eaves, and the leaves whispered as the wind blew them while I sat on the porch. I would lean out of the bedroom windows, look up into the sunshine, let the glow hit me in my face, feel the air, and bask in my happiness. I would read and then lie on the porch, looking up into the sky; imagination took me to such beautiful places.

I spent a lots of my days trying to make the best of my life, when things were on an even keel (no one swearing, fighting, or crying). These were the days I would spend on the porch, because the neighbours would not be an audience for my family's performances. Yes, drama happened a lot on my street because most people were poor and facing similar dilemmas.

Every time there was an argument, it was entertainment for the rest of the street, with people gawking out of their windows or going into the street to get a better view.

On my sunny and peaceful days, I could pretend all was normal. Sometimes I would sit and think of all the people I had encountered so far in my life, and how they had affected me. I was grateful I spent time with some, and then I was truly regretful of wasting precious time with others. But again, I have learnt valuable life lessons from all my mistakes. The valuable lessons and the people I encountered will be shared with you as we go along.

I can tell you of my pet Panda, a kitten I adopted when she wandered into the yard. She was black and white with a limp to one of her back legs. We had several stray animals who would wander into our yard. Fences kept nothing out and were just there for decorative reasons; usually they were old and falling apart.

Panda knew when I was sad and would jump onto my lap, purring and making me feel loved. This was a kitten I fell in love with and still miss. She was so cute and had a way of looking into my soul. I think she was there for me as a blessing through my toughest years growing up. However, I did not have her around as long as I wanted. My neighbours always had fish drying in the sun on racks. Panda, being a cat, would sometimes take a few bites. They beat the poor little kitty. When we found Panda, she could barely crawl; she was severely beaten and bleeding. My love for pets ended because it hurt too much to care so much for a pet, knowing that it wouldn't last forever. I could not stand the pain. Still, Panda was the best!

Now, let's get back to my family. It was hard seeing my parents always angry and arguing over money. I decided to dream and wish for lots of money; maybe this would take away all their worries. I became so consumed with my self-pity and with trying to pretend it all away. I truly wanted my parents to be happy and not experience pain and suffering. Arguments would flare up between my parents out of desperation and disappointment. I think my dad was so ashamed of his failures that he took it out on my mom. I sometimes could not take it, and I would cry and shout at my dad to stop yelling at my mom. Then my mom would tell me to not interfere, saying it was not my place to tell my dad anything. I would get confused because I only wanted him to stop hurting her, and I wanted her to be happy. Later in life, I understood she wanted to protect me.

My brothers sometimes wanted to interject too, but that never ended well. I remember this one time when my older brother, Anthony, got protective of my mom during a really bad argument. My dad chased him with a huge knife, then my mom grabbed all of us, and we stood outside our home, shivering with fear. Passersby saw the tears and fear on our faces. To me, it was surreal, and I felt like there was a parallel world outside of mine where no one could really see us, but we could see out. I guess this was my way of protecting myself, shielding the world from my life, and pretending that no one else could see or hear the craziness. We were all crazed out of our minds. My mom started begging for my dad to stop and let us in. She cried profusely and wanted my dad to stop so we could go in and not be publicly humiliated. I was so scared that I did not want to go back in – I wanted to run. But I was frozen, and my mind seemed to have stop thinking. I remember it as if it was yesterday.

I was scared and then confused when, after a few hours, my dad and mom made up and everyone seemed to be okay. Maybe in my mind it was worse than it actually had been? I grew up and realized that coping mechanisms for everyone are different; what seems normal to some may not quite be the same for folks stuck in a quagmire. My brothers were hardly ever home, and at the time I never understood why. I thought it was perfectly normal to stay at home all day during summer and after school, being indoors, reading, and not getting into my parents' way. My brothers took advantage of the fact that they were allowed to go out without permission; they avoided the madhouse with my father's temperament and his abuse of my poor mother. To this day, I still do not know how and why my mom took all of the suffering she did, but I do know that I admire her for staying sane and not taking it out on me. As I got older, I realized it was unbearable being home; my parents effectively drove away my brothers. Eventually I would leave too.

I learnt how to introspect very early and honed that skill to perfection. By the time I was a teenager, no one knew what was going on in my mind. Some people thought I was not very smart because I was not an active participant in conversations and emotions. I was not stupid, and in my own opinion, I was smart enough to understand and react to things. Sometimes I was over-analytical to the point where it was a pain, being able to examine in detail every thought or person who came into my life. No one ever seemed to fit my criteria of an ideal person (until I got older and realized that some of the best people in my life had already crossed my path, but I was too stupid to be cognizant of these values). My personality bordered on two extremes. I tried to be really exciting to fit in with people I felt were important to be around, and I was really boring with those who valued me the most, spending no energy trying to be happy or nice. I was a flip-flop of emotions and logic.

I miss my dad because he was primarily instrumental for my unconventional thoughts and knowledge, even with all that he had done to my mom. Sometimes we still love those who suffer from visible defects, whether physical or psychological.

I think because my mom never really discussed anything after each argument with us, my brothers and I always pretended that these events never happened. It made life more bearable, or at least we pretended it did. The reality was too harsh, even for my mom. However, I think we suffered from repression, being unable to express due to the energy spent on pretending.

My mom suffered the most because she was the victim by all definitions. She would sit and cry buckets, her face drawn and old; even at the age of forty, all the plumpness of life had been sucked out of her. My mom was so pretty in my eyes, and I could not stand to see her unhappy. I started the love-hate relationship with my dad. I loved that he tried his best in his own way to be a good dad, but I hated him for all the things he did to my mom.

Now, look at me. My life is not half as bad; however, things have happened to me that make me feel dirty inside, chewed up, and sometimes so small that I think about hiding away from it all. But we all experience bad things in our lives, and we all survive and move on. Some do it better than others.

Why should life be as hard as this? This is the question I still ask myself as I sit and think. Life sometimes has a way of fixing itself, if we could only abide with the consequences until all the sorting out is done! Sometimes we can control the harshness of life, but some issues are inevitable. Still, we survive, learn how to cope with our continued existence, and sometimes come out on top!

When I was ten, I realized that I was destined to become great, though I was not sure why or how. I always had the feeling that I would either die or have a life-changing experience at the age of twenty-four. I always had weird premonitions, most of which came true; some were visualized, and others were vaguely connected.

Chapter 4

Growing Pains

Circumstances can make or break people. I have learnt throughout my life that it is always up to the person to make a choice. There is always a choice even when we think there is not. We simply need to think about everything in detail. First we clear our heads, and then we shape our lives. It also takes a lot of introspection. You will have to look at yourself honestly, and then you will know what you are truly capable of doing, accepting, and changing.

Brad was funny, and he would always try to visualise imaginary things. I remember him telling me, "Imagine the world using buttons instead of money." As a seamstress, my mom had lots of buttons, so that would have made us rich. He was very protective towards me. I remember when I was at St Mary's Elementary School, and we were at recess. I was very introverted at that age, and I simply stood there, not really chatting or anything. Two girls were chasing each other and running really fast. One bowled me over, and my lips were cut and bleeding from the impact.

My brother was playing with a group of boys because he was very social. He saw what had happened and came running over to console me. He took me over to the tap nearby, washed my face, and hugged me. He was crying when he saw all the blood. He loved me very much, and he stayed with me until our mom came for us after school.

Those were really good days. I remember my mom coming at lunchtime and taking us to sit on the steps outside of the huge, old church across the road. Sometimes we went into the church and prayed; it was quiet, beautiful, and so full of light. I always felt good when we were in the churchyard. Brad, Mom, and I would sit closely together and put our food on the steps, eating and enjoying the shade as the sunlight played on the leaves and trees. The air was so clean, and being there with my mom and brother made me happy. But sadly, this changed because I was not tough enough to survive in the school.

I went to a different school shortly after that, and Brad stayed at St Mary, creating a gap between us. I lived in my own world at my new school, too shy to make friends and too scared to speak. I also missed Brad terribly. I never knew why my parents did not try to make more of an effort to keep us together, because I would have liked that. I looked at the other girls and wanted their pretty barrettes, fancy school bags, and pretty shoes. I wanted to be picked up by a fancy mom smelling of flowers and wearing make-up and high-heeled shoes. I think this was when I started being ashamed of my life, my mom, and what I was. This was the school my dad had tried so hard to get me into, the school of the privileged.

I never knew what my mom gave me was worth more than all the exterior glamour and riches. My mom always put me first and made all my clothes; she took the time to make sure I never knew everything that went on in the home. I know she was busy and tired, and she never spoke to me about life. I know she didn't prepare me for growing up, and sometimes I went hungry, but I am sure that she never knew these things were missing because she never got treated any better growing up.

Or at least she thought I didn't because I never said anything. I hardly spoke, which I didn't realize at the time. I had so many thoughts going on in my head, and I always imagined my words were vocal and not just happening in my mind. I suppressed a lot of feelings and tried my best to outwardly show happiness.

This school was fancy, and the children were rich and beautiful. I thought of myself as dirty and poor, and I never figured I was anything but plain. My life was focused on learning, reading, and studying the children around me. I found it rather easy to learn, even with hardly any food or beverages. My mom tried her hardest to always pack something in my lunch kit, such as a boiled egg or fried potatoes. I was too ashamed to open my lunch kit and eat my snacks or lunch in front of the others. The few times I did, the other children either made fun of my food or took my food and ate it. I went hungry most days, and I wanted the day to end. I found it unbearable to be at school, yet I somehow managed to keep abreast with the schoolwork and got great results on tests. I always waited for my mom to come get me, and on our walk home, I became at peace and happy.

Funny enough, during the last year at school, I got accustomed to being there amongst children. Even though I didn't really play, I felt like I was part of all that was happening, and everything seemed so sunny and bright. It seemed by then I was not such an outstanding cast-off.

I made a few friends, and they were good to me and never made fun of me. They made me feel normal and accepted me as I was. At least, I thought so, but really they were just being kind to me. I never got invited to any of their parties, nor did they keep in contact with me after school. Children only did as they were told. I am sure now that their parents did not want me around them after school. These children were just being polite and well mannered.

Mind you, there were some memories I have that made the days spent at this school seem fun, like swinging and playing. It was fun having time to be a child; all my worries would float away, and I was as light as the clouds floating overhead. My heart felt as bright as the sun flitting through the clouds.

A few months after I had started at St Margaret's, I was sitting quietly in class. As I had been doing for all my eight years, I was talking to myself in my mind, unaware that I needed to also speak aloud. While I sat there thinking away and feeling happy, the teacher was discussing science; I forget what about. I was jolted out of my reverie when Mrs Brown called my name and asked me a question.

For the life of me, I thought I had been listening, but I guess that's how introverts think and feel. With the question she asked, I drew blanks and had absolutely no idea what she was talking about. The class snickered, and I felt like I could disappear. I stood there and was mute, which was interpreted as rudeness, so the teacher met with my dad and had a chat. My dad asked me why I did not answer. I cannot remember if I said anything in response; I simply knew that I would remember that day.

In another class the next school year, all I remember was being the only child with a brown paper bag for a schoolbag, and looking at the other children with envy. I think my teacher told my mom I was made fun of by the other children, and the school wanted to know why I had a paper bag. My mom got some materials from somewhere and sewed a bag for me. It was quite pretty, and I kept it clean and was proud of it. I remember one nasty little girl who always brought the coolest snacks, and she would offer these to a few children who were as snooty as she. Needless to say, she never offered me any. The third thing I remember was that there was a really pretty girl, and I cannot remember how we started communicating, but we borrowed books from each other. She refused to return one, I became upset, and she hit me. I never told my parents and took the scolding for the missing book. I never understood why children were mean, and it still mystifies me. Why do people feel the need to be mean? What does it do for them? I would eventually learn as these children grow up, sometimes they changed, but sometimes they got worse.

I guess when we are more fortunate than others, we take things for granted, and we think those without are lesser than us. Truthfully, we are all on the same level when it comes to survival. But that's a different story, right?

Then came the summers in between the school years. I did lots of reading so time could pass by without me having to be part of it. I sat by the window if my mom had to leave me home alone, never budging an inch and jumping out of my skin at every sound or movement within or outside. This was when I grew fond of watching people; I found it fascinating, and time would fly by with this activity. I didn't even think of eating, drinking, or even going to the washroom. I am sure I sat there so many days for hours because I was left alone a lot. Goodness knows how long I stood by the window, staring out at people. I was so petrified that I became paranoid to even turn my head. When my mom returned home, I would run as fast as I could to open the door before the boogie man took hold of me. My heart would then start beating again (at least, that's what it felt like each time, as if time stood still and I had not breathed until my mom's return). I am not sure why my mom never took me with her. I cannot even begin to assume and give way to my imagination, which seems to lead in so many different directions.

Another school year passed, and I was eleven, going into the last year before heading to high school. I was a year younger than most of the other children in my class. I remember lots about this class because I think I started awakening from my slumber.

I remember my first day and seeing all the children entirely. They weren't just a snooty girl and a pretty girl, a really handsome boy or a rather fat boy – I saw all of them in their entirety. I didn't categorize much, and I made a few more friends. This was where I made friends with two really nice girls and boys.

I sat on the right-hand side of the class. The middle was segmented into two columns, eight rows across and two side columns, I sat in the right column. My neighbours were David Rob and Gretel Green, and in front of me sat Gerry Narry and Vitty Kidd. Gretel and David were troublemakers, so I'm not quite sure why I was lumped with them, unless it was because I was so poor and dirty that I had to be tucked away. Or perhaps the teacher did not want to be bothered by me? These were the best seats in the classroom because we were away from all the other children but were on the outside of the classroom.

I liked a few of the other girls for my friends, but at first I was too shy. Somehow they became my friends because they approached me. I was very smart and aced all the tests, but like Gerry, I was very shy and did not like the being in the spotlight.

This is a really good memory – good in that it's clear, but not great because it was embarrassing. I remember one more thing about the previous school year. I was so quiet that the teacher thought I had a problem, like I was mute. One day Vitty was loud and didn't care if he was fat or not; he was happy with who he was! I think I learnt a bit from him about how to like myself.

With this incident, he cleared the classroom when the teacher said she was stepping out for a while, and she would be back in an hour. Vitty was put in charge. He made a makeshift stage with the chairs and tables, and he proceeded modelling. Madness and excitement must have gotten into me, because I suddenly grabbed an imaginary mike and started speaking into it. "Here comes Vitty, all shiny and bright, posing and modelling for you today!" I must have been really loud. The class was clapping and engaged, and I felt happy. This was the only time I remembered being out of my shell.

Suddenly there was a hush, and I looked back to the door of the classroom, where the teacher stood there in disbelief – not at Vitty, but at me! I didn't know what to do. I kind of slouched and hid behind the other students, but she would not have any of it. She came marching up to me and said in front of the class, "Amber, you do not answer any questions and never speak in class. I thought something was wrong with you. And here you are screaming away! You will never be quiet again, and when I speak to you, you will speak up!" I remember being embarrassed, and I wanted the floor to open up and swallow me. I forget what happened next as I shut down and went back to quiet mode.

Let's return to the next school year, where everything seemed promising, and I have more memories to talk about. David and Gretel were so much fun, but sometimes they were not so good to have around because they got into trouble for talking. One day my teacher called out my name, and I had to stand in front of the class, where I got a good few hits in the palm of my hand with a cane. I cried, and when I got home, I showed my mom. She was most upset and went into school the next day to have a discussion with the teacher.

My mom always believed in me and never thought I was capable of getting into trouble. My mom talked to the teacher, and I am not sure what she said, but I never again got caned or made fun of. Did David and Gretel get into trouble? No. You see, these were children from very rich parents who generously contributed to the school every year.

I got great grades in this last class because I was aware of all that was going on, and I was excited by the possibilities. I digested everything my teacher projected, whether it was sewing or mathematics. The favourite subject was aptitude, where it was up to the individual to figure out answers using math or language skills.

I borrowed a lot of books from the other children and was getting so integrated that I even started a viable profit-making trade business. I got lots of cool stickers from my mom, who started going to the neighbouring countries to buy goods and sell them back for a profit. One of the items was stickers.

I know it sounds silly, but she made decent money from the sales of the stickers, and this was only one of her items. She bought lingerie, clothing, and even some foodstuff that was not for sale in our country and was contraband. However, so many people had the same idea, and all at the same time, so demand became lower than the supply. Soon this business produced a loss for my parents.

But back to my business. Mom gave me the stickers that she could not sell. I started using these stickers as a ploy to entice children at school to give me books in exchange for a certain amount of stickers, and boy, did I build a good-sized library – until one girl's mom became upset and told her it was not a fair exchange. She was my best customer because her parents bought her books written by Hans Christian Andersen and other good authors. Soon, everyone else became less interested, and I stopped my trading. I think my mom also told me not to because she didn't want me getting into trouble at school with the teachers and children. I did stop, but I like to think it was my decision.

Later in the school year, I got to know two really cool girls, Lisa and Marie. These were the coolest kids in class, and they seemed to genuinely like me. I thought they were the coolest kids because they were popular, pretty, and liked by everyone. It seemed so easy for them to make friends, and they were always smiling.

Lisa came over one day and said, "So where do you live?" I answered, and apparently she lived in the same neighbourhood; so did Marie. They were cousins, but I learnt this long afterwards. We started walking home together, and sometimes I would go by Marie's house. Marie had two older sisters, and they were a riot and so full of life.

One day I really wanted to go to the washroom, but I didn't know how to ask. I was truly an introvert, or even a little strange. I never said anything, even though Marie invited me in and offered me a beverage. I drank and was still was fine after, but oh my goodness, here comes another vivid memory!

We went outside on the veranda, where I sat in a hammock. Her eldest sister, Karen, came over and pretended she was someone else. Then her sister Susie came over and started tickling me. They tickled and tickled, and my bladder felt like it would explode!

I kept it in and thought all was fine – until when I was leaving, *whoosh,* it came splashing around me like a balloon bursting. Pee went into my socks and shoes and drenched my tunic. I felt so bad. What to do and where to go when in such a predicament, where your friend and her sisters saw everything?

I ran and sloshed all the way home. The sun was so hot that most of it dried up until only my shoes were soaked when I got home. I lied to my mom that I'd stepped into a waterhole. She looked at me, not believing but not sure what to say. I think she knew I had peed myself! I was so ashamed that I avoided Marie for months after, and I never went back to her home.

I started hanging out with Lisa more and more, and we became best friends. Lisa was really nice and taught me some things I still carry with me. She was fun and naughty and never judged me. She was never ashamed to be seen with me, and she liked me as I was. It was such a great feeling to have a friend who really liked me! I still hung out with Marie but always felt ashamed around her.

School was fun in the last year. There was so much to learn and so much to do, with lots of extracurricular activities. This was the last year of elementary, before going into high school. I was becoming a big girl. I had friends now, and I had fun with them. I remember playing a game called jacks. It has a little ball with objects with spikes, which you grab as the ball bounces once. Then you pick up the objects, increasing in number, and you grab the ball at the same time. I got really good at this game. I played this with Marie and Lisa. We would walk home, stop at bus stops, and play jacks for a while. Then we would slowly make our way home. The funny thing is, I cannot remember my parents asking me why I was late. Maybe they were not always even at home. I would put away my school bag, take any books I'd borrowed, and curl up in a chair. Time would pass me by without me being aware of anything.

I remember my family moving several times before we ended up in a little town called Kettle. We stayed there for a few years, moving houses within the same town during our stay.

Why did we have to move so often? Well, let's see how my memories are. I remember living in another town called Nebton, in a house with people who lived in the same house. We lived downstairs, and my mom would go out. I'm not sure where; I think for groceries and to sell the clothes she made. I was very little then; this is as far back as my memory goes, to the first few places we lived. I would stay with whomever my mom left me with and refused any food or drink. I'd not talk, and sometimes I'd lose control of my bladder. I was too scared to talk. I must have been a really strange child to have around. I was also too little to be left with complete strangers. I can remember being small, scared, and stressed. I still wonder where my mom would go.

Anyway, back to moving. In Nebton, my dad went out a lot with his teacher friends and with some other friends from the local customs and regulations company he worked at before he became a teacher. One day, my mom and I were returning home from somewhere, and I saw my dad lying in the walkway. I ran to him, but my mom was faster and ordered me to stay out whilst she tried to get him to move. He was as drunk as a skunk! He was lying prone on the concrete ground, his clothes were in a mess, and he was as stinky as could be. Oh, the argument they had! It was terrible, but I think my dad started to drink less. He was weak, and I think he couldn't cope with life's difficulties. We always struggled for money, and he would take it out on Mom or go drinking with his buddies.

After a while, we could not pay the rent, so the people who lived upstairs, who were also the landlords, started confronting my parents. My dad was never one to accept blame, and he retaliated by being verbally abusive. My dad was never compromising and would get defensive and angry.

I think of all the days when I would feel so ashamed that we were poor and that no one seemed to like us. I felt a bit like *The Little Match Girl*, looking in another world that was filled with wonderment and that seemed so out of reach.

I think when a child grows up in an environment where there are constant arguments, there are tons of internal conflict and confusion, creating a lack of self-confidence. I did feel rather bereft and not quite part of the normal world most of the time. I never knew why, but I always felt badly afterwards, as if my world was even darker and that something else would happen that was really awful. I still have that foreboding feeling whenever I am experiencing conflict or am stuck in an uncomfortable situation. Maybe this is because I always had to deal with unpleasantness growing up, and so every time I feel all is going well, I wait for the inevitable bad thing to happen.

After the arguments and confrontations, we had to move and had nowhere to go, because we had no money. We moved to my grandpa's home in the countryside. I remember coming home after a walk with my parents, and all our belongings were thrown on the street! My parents were horrified and then angry. My brothers were out and did not have to see all this. My parents started yelling at the landlord, and people were passing and staring. I could feel myself shrinking smaller and smaller, wanting to be invisible.

We moved to my grandpa's immediately, after my parents went looking for my brothers. My brothers were bewildered, but that didn't say much. We went along with whatever our parents did. My grandpa was my mother's dad; my grandma had passed away. I thought maybe this was not such a bad thing, because my grandpa would now have us, and we could look after him.

I was excited, because I had spent time by my grandparents before. Reflecting on it now, I realize why it was so welcoming: this was because I got away from my parents and their perpetual worries. When I went on vacation, I played all day long, and most of the time I was alone in the yard because it was safe. The yard was huge with so many hiding places and things to do. My world was fanciful, and I escaped through imagination when I stayed with my grandparents.

There were so many fruit trees and coconut trees, with branches covering most of the sky in the backyard, making it nice and cool all day long; it was like a magic place away from everything. Then there were mango trees with so many mangoes, cherry trees, guava trees, and a few more. I remember my grandpa was so good with his hands; he grafted trees and flowers and created fusion fruit trees and exotic colours never seen before. It was the envy of the neighbourhood.

His planting area was at the front of the yard, where he enclosed all his prize flowers and plants, including ferns of all shapes and sizes and beautiful flowers. If I close my eyes, I can still imagine being there. I would sneak into this forbidden secret garden, sit under the plants, and stay there for hours, feeling safe and at peace.

It was so perfect. I was so looking forward to us moving in with my grandpa. I did not think that anything bad would happen, and I could not have foreseen what came next. I still was too young to fully realize just how weird adults are, always spoiling things that are pure and magical. We are malicious creatures and are deadly, masters of our own destiny and owners of our own demise.

CHAPTER 5

LIFE IN THE COUNTRYSIDE

My dolls were the closest things to friends and were my solace, along with reading when things got really rough in the house. Speaking of houses, I told you how we were like nomads. We had moved and moved again, and every time I thought this was part of my life: I would get accustomed to a place, and then it was time to move. The eternal struggle for money always brought with it lots of heated arguments between my parents, and lots of places to move to. Sometimes we were unable to pay rent and were evicted.

Thank goodness for my mom's parents. They had a little cottage in the countryside, and without them, most likely the entire family would have been homeless and on the streets. My grandfather adored me, and my grandmother tolerated me. At the time of moving, sadly my grandma was no longer there. I was unaware of just how much my dad hated my grandfather, and it had to be the point of no return for us to move in with him. My grandfather took us in with open arms, yet my dad never thanked my grandfather. I truly have no bad memories of my grandfather; he was so good to me. He was a tough guy but was rather soft with me.

When we got to my grandpa's house, I was the first one out of the truck. Our scant belongings, few bits of furniture, and items were packed inside. The neighbours were gawking, and quite a few gathered to discuss this new event in their village. I didn't care because I was excited to be moving into the cottage.

My brothers followed at a much slower pace and with a lot of gruff, especially my oldest brother. Anthony had not complained when told we had to move; however, I knew he had his gang in Nebton, and he had started taking drugs and listening to heavy metal. I knew he was upset that he was moving away from them. My dad was so keen on him growing into a macho guy, with the concept that boys should have their freedom. My dad would not see the error of his parenting methods even when things got worse for my brother.

Even though Brad was not as grumpy, I knew that he had been close to my grandma and not my grandpa, so I guess it was not the same for him. Also, I knew that he had a lot on his mind, which was too much for him. I really should have reached out to him, but again, being younger, I didn't have the wisdom.

Once we got settled, things seemed better at first. I would still be left home, but I had my grandpa, so I didn't mind. I would go about, doing things like walking around the yard and enjoying the trees and flowers. My mind would sometimes flit into fantasyland, and I would imagine fairies and magical creatures. Sometimes while sitting on the stairs, my mind would be flooded with memories of my grandma before she got sick and passed away. She was vibrant, petite, dark, and an awesome cook. She liked me, but not the same way that she liked Brad. When we stayed there during the summer, I remember her feeding him (he was maybe ten) and ignoring me. I had food too, just not the attention.

Don't get me wrong, she did love me. She taught me many things, such as how to braid hair, and how there are so many ways of using tamarind, which I fell in love with. I'm still not sure if it's considered a fruit or vegetable, but it's used in so many ways. My grandma would swiftly skin a huge basket of tamarind and put it up on the roof during the day for the sun to cook it. She would boil tamarind and make a sauce. If you had a cold and drank it, the cold would go away. She also did the same things to other fruits. My grandma taught me how to peel shrimp and clean fish. I also learnt how to sweep and mop. She bought me really nice snacks from the local market, which is something I need to describe.

Every day at 11 a.m., vendors in the countryside would bring their goods and place them in makeshift stalls to sell. By 2 p.m., everyone would be done and ready to leave for their homes. Saturdays were the best because vendors came from elsewhere, and it was busier with so many more things. I remember the toys, fruits, vegetables, fish, chicken, snacks, freshly made beverages, and noise from everyone talking, seemed like music to me then. Children ran around whilst their moms shopped. The men who worked during the week were mostly at home, relaxing or doing yard work, except for the men who worked in the market. The sun would stream into the stalls and make everything look pretty and delicious.

My grandma had me loiter around when she was cooking, so I could learn. She would make me this special bread that was truly awesome. She was more patient with me when she was cooking.

Somehow she also did things to aggravate my dad. My dad did not like too many people, and sometimes I think I am quite like him, made up of both the good and bad characteristics.

My dad got upset with almost everything my grandparents did, and he sometimes got upset with them in a way that I never understood. Thinking back, I can now see a pattern: my dad got upset with people and argued a lot. He had no patience with anyone and felt that he knew more than everyone else.

I think secretly, my grandma wanted to annoy him. She would sometimes buy sugar candy (these were called this because it was 100 per cent sugar). My dad would get mad with her, and in turn she would get upset and cry, saying that all she wanted to do was to make me happy. I remember feeling sad and confused; I didn't think my grandma was doing anything wrong. I also loved my dad. But I really wanted those sweets. After the dust settled, I would sneak the sweets into a hideaway spot and eat almost all of them in one sitting!

My brothers continued going out and were never around. Anthony seemed like he was never there during my younger years.

My grandpa was a handsome fellow. I remember always looking at him with awe. He seemed so formidable and strong. He was very muscular, and he loved spending time with his plants, doing yard work and building things. Truth be told, he was so self-sufficient that he'd built the house all by himself. He did everything for himself. I knew that his way of life made him happy in his own way, and he never seemed to need anything. What a way to live! We all envy people who can find oneness, but sometimes it is not that difficult. If we were not as materialistic and could be content with simple things in life, living humbly, perhaps we all could find that space that makes us feel just right.

We moved in, and things seemed fine for a few days. Maybe I was too busy enjoying the sunshine, trees, birds, animals, and the life happening around me. I mentioned my dad creating conflicts and not liking anyone. He seemed a bit paranoid and did some very irrational things. His hate for my grandpa grew, and I thought that there was a constant battle of wills to see who was more manly and in charge. My dad did not see the whole picture. This was my grandpa's home, and he had lived there all his married life.

My father did not treat my grandpa nicely. I got upset and confused because I loved them both. My mom got caught in the middle; she was a wife and a daughter. Dad made her choose. It was not fair because my mom is a wonderful, loving, beautiful woman, and I love her very much. She made everything seem so much better by trying her best to treat everyone fairly. My poor mom ended up doing things so that my dad felt this was his home, and my poor grandpa had to take a back seat. How that must have hurt him; he was so self-reliant, and this was his world. Suddenly my dad was the dominant male, and my grandpa was no longer significant – he was a castaway at best. I feel so guilty thinking about this, and I will always feel this way. I think even then, I may have been able to stand up for my grandpa and help him live the rest of his years in a much happier state.

There were many fruits trees, so I was never really hungry. I loved living there, and I would get up really early on Saturdays to wash dishes, scrub the floors, clean the house, and sweep the yard because I wanted everything neat and clean before I had a shower (which was a bucket of water and soap). I would push away the thoughts of my grandpa in the recesses of my mind, and I'd focus on the things that made me happy.

After showering, I would get a snack (cut-up mangoes with salt and pepper – real pepper), get a book, lie on the front veranda with a pillow and a sheet, and enjoy being outdoors. With the sun and sky in view, I'd immerse myself into my book. This was the life! The clouds would float above my head, and I would get lost in the world, floating away with the soft, wispy, feathery, and imaginative creatures found in the sky. It was a good feeling. I remember enjoying these moments even more when my brothers were not home and my parents were busy with other things. It was my own little world, and I would escape into my book and sometimes fall asleep.

I loved also being in the hammock downstairs when my grandpa was not in it. On weekends he would sometimes go for walks and be with his friends. He had pretty birds he kept in cages, and he would feed them and train them to whistle. When he and his friends were together, they would have competitions with their birds. He loved being active, and I am quite like him.

My grandpa and I would go for long walks along the seashore, walking on the beaches. Each morning he would fill a huge sack with sand and carry it on his back all the way home. He would then laboriously lay the sand all over his garden and also over his yard. He did this every day. I think this is why his yard was so rich and fertile, and all the plants, flowers, and fruits were unique and wonderful. He spent almost all his day doing yard work, and when he was tired, he'd lay in his hammock. Can you see why he was my idol growing up? He did everything for himself, relied on no one, and was fine with himself as he was. He didn't have to measure up to someone's standards, and he had no games to play. His was a simple way of life, unfettered.

My favourite was when we would go to collect his pension, and he would treat me to snacks, which I would eat up. He loved me so much and told me so. He would say, "You are my favourite grandchild. The others are no good." That was so nice to hear. I looked up to my grandpa, and he made me feel important. That is strange because he was really tough and didn't smile or talk too much. He never hugged or kissed me. Of all my cousins and brothers, all of his grandchildren, he didn't like any of them except me. He told me that they were only nice to him so that he'd give them things like gifts and money.

My neighbours seemed nice, at least for the first year after we'd moved in. There were so many children and so many yards to play in, and my parents allowed me to play with the children … until trouble brewed. My dad had to stir it all up. When I think back, he truly was intolerant of people, and he didn't treat anyone well, not even my mom. It showed in his speech and his expressions. Sometimes I think he didn't like my brothers. I guess he loved them, but he didn't show it the way he should have. He was quite paranoid and thought that the entire world was conspiring to cast evil into his life. My dad somehow indicated to all the neighbours that we were better than them and that they were either ignorant (as in stupid) or were no good. The neighbours started avoiding my mom, gossiping and getting mad, and the children were not allowed to play with me.

Still, I will talk about before all of this happened, so you can see that all was not dismal and I did have fun. I try to always remember the good, because this is what keeps all of us going in our lives. I played with Tracey and Natasha a lot; they lived across the road from us. Given how the houses were set up, it was almost as if we could see into each other's rooms and windows. They went to my school, which was a bonus, so we would go to school and come home together. They also understood how to play board games and read, so it was fun playing with them. They were smart and pretty, and I really liked them.

We would play hide and seek at home, or we would play in their yard, which was cooler. They were fairly well off and had nicer furniture and a pretty house. I didn't realize at that time that they liked my home better because the yard was bigger and there were so many neat places and trees.

We also played with another girl named Daisy. She was a bit strange, always gave me sour looks, and never was nice to me. I think she was jealous of me playing with Natasha and Tracey; somehow she thought I stole her friends from her.

It was also fun playing house, using dolls and pretending we were adults. I thought it was finally fun to play with other children and not have to be by myself.

We would also lend each other books and spend time together chatting or just being. I loved going over by them because their house was so much nicer and bigger. Soon this would change against my wishes.

My parents somehow seemed to be unhappy with the time I spent there, and they made me feel guilty about playing, as if I was doing something wrong. With my oversized conscience, I stopped playing with the girls. To please my parents, I avoided any conflict.

I became sad and lonely. It seemed that for my parents, protecting me meant that I stayed at home all the time unless I went out with them or was at school. I did not know how lonely I was, and I felt quite at peace with myself, reading lots, cleaning the house, and creating ways to be busy and feel wanted. My dad was jealous of my time with other people, as he then thought I was happier with them – which I was, but I had to obey him. I didn't know anything else.

My favourite topic at school was literature because I got to read lots of books and project my interpretations as part of the lesson. I was somewhat of an introvert, so my teacher made me read aloud to the class quite often. It was not a punishment; I knew she wanted me to climb out of my hiding place and be more expressive. Soon I enjoyed being able to stand in the classroom and read aloud, with everyone listening raptly as I became part of the story and emoted the words. I would get so engrossed in my school books that all homework seemed enjoyable. Sometimes I didn't know whether I ate my dinner or not; time seemed to slip by rather quickly.

I remember my grandpa lying in his hammock and smelling of sweat; he was always puttering around in his yard, gardening. The hammock smelled of him. I thought it was a rather pleasant smell and would jump into the hammock as soon as he left it. I know it doesn't sound rather attractive, but I felt closer to my grandpa this way.

My brothers never were at home, so life didn't change for them. They continued the same routine and behaviour as before. My parents were still so busy scraping for money and running around. I am not sure where they got money from, because I never thought of asking. I was always thinking instead of speaking aloud. I figured Mom sold clothes she sewed, and my father went along to accompany her. I learnt later in life that this was a lot more complicated.

My dad became even more frustrated as time went by and money became harder to get. Even with no rent to pay, he still had to provide for all of us. My older brother worked but kept the money. I don't know what my younger brother did during those years. I think he was pretty messed up at this stage and had his escape from reality by doing things that made his life seem glamorous. I know he lied to his friends about our lives and our home, and he made it sound as if he was from a wealthy family. He kept hanging out with older, rich friends.

Each of us was so consumed by individual thoughts and ways of coping with life's difficulties that we had not been a family for years, until it became too late. I remember happier days when we were living in Newton. Both my brothers were younger, and even though this was rare, we did go out on weekends and spend time together at home. When we moved, this stopped.

The people in the countryside learnt to hate us and envy us at the same time. They hated my father, especially because he created arguments and made them feel inferior. They had envy because we seemed different and well-spoken, and our mannerisms seemed more refined.

The people my mom grew up with invited us to several outings, weddings, and religious functions, and my mom would take me. I loved going to these because the food was splendid, and the music and excitement was pure happiness for me. It also gave me a chance to be around people. My life seemed to be contained within our home, and I had to ensure that I played my radio quietly; the boys got yelled at if they played the radio was too loud, or even if the music was not acceptable, such as heavy metal, which I grew to like. It's really angry, emotional music, but it provides an outlet for expressions and emotions.

Anthony was really into drugs by now, and I don't quite know how my parents did not detect it at this stage. Maybe they never had the time to pay attention. He was irrational, was always absent, and played heavy metal any chance he got. If my dad was not home, he would turn up the radio loudly, and then he upgraded by getting a cassette player. He was a teenager with no boundaries, and he took it as far as he could.

I do not remember seeing Anthony around a lot. I have fewer visual memories of him as a teenager than I do of Brad. I only remember seeing him at family occasions and religious functions, and hearing him get yelled at whenever he was home. When he played his music, I wanted to listen because this was my chance to have something in common with him. I felt that I never really got a chance to know either of my two brothers.

It seemed that everything my older brother did irked my dad, though I am still not sure why. My dad retaliated to our taste of music by getting his religious cassettes, and then he would play these loudly early in the mornings, especially on weekends. This was torture for us, but to him, this was parenting and teaching his children traditional values; somehow, listening to this music would make us cleansed and religious. He grew up with the mindset that no one should sleep when the sun had fully risen; we should be awake before that. It was some superstition he grew up with. I doubt Dad ever had a clean mind. How come wherever we lived, no one liked us? How come he would get into arguments with all the neighbours, and how come he always felt the need to one-up everyone?

My brothers would grumble when my dad played his music, and they would have no choice but to get up because Dad would get really mad at them. I think after some time, they tried to keep peace when they could to avoid a confrontation and commotion.

I think my favourite time of my life while growing up was in the countryside, but this special time was before we lived there, when I visited my grandparents during the summer and did not have my parents with me. My time with my grandparents offered me the space to grow as a child, explore my imagination, and get lost in my thoughts.

I still tried to do the things I did when I spent my vacations there, but things changed over the years we lived there. Things became real.

Chapter 6

Things Changing

My grandpa became older and more reliant on my mom to do things for him as time passed by. I tried to help, but in my mind, I think I lived in an alternate world. People talk about a place they go to hide when something truly bad is happening to them. I think I became an expert at this in order to survive, and yet I'd appear normal in my everyday life.

I went to school and was seemingly happy, always smiling. Soon I received the nickname Fresco. I did not mind because I liked that brand of toothpaste, but some of the other children thought it made fun of me and used it that way.

I think I was pretty in a weird, nerdish way. I tried my best to always be clean and neat, and I loved to dress up. Though I was limited in fancy items, I always did my hair in different styles. I would read magazines, studying pictures to emulate the hairstyles. I also was not skinny, but I was healthy looking. I did not get too much to eat, so even if I ate a huge bag of sweets, I didn't have to think about consequences. Because I introspected a lot, I think I also became quite mature in my thinking, and I did quite well with my studies.

I must have been rather boring. Actually, a few of my friends have told me that I was. Once I grew up, I tried to keep in contact with quite a few of my old friends, but these relationships never really flourished. I had thought of these people as my friends, but I think they'd simply tolerated my presence because I was quiet and didn't intrude in their lives. However, none of them thought of me as exciting, fun to be with, or a cool friend. I now find that I am truly bored being around them as their conversations are not interesting enough to keep me engaged. I wanted so badly to hang out with all the awesome children and be part of the gang. I wanted them to accept me, and then I would become someone. Little did I know that I stood out like a sore thumb.

Bigger things were happening at the same time. I was questioning my value on earth, and things were changing at home. My father became more vocal about his concerns regarding my grandpa, and he wanted me to have my grandpa's room because I was sharing a room with my two brothers. One of them was on drugs, and the other was still within the realm of normalcy.

I try not to portray Dad as a monster, but truth be told, there were some instances in my life where I felt like he became a different person, a complete stranger, and he did horrible things to everyone. He wanted me in a different room because my older brother had a propensity (bordering on abuse) to request I kiss or hug him, and I felt repulsed to even hug him. As I got older, I figured he was a mess and was perverted. I still get confused in my mind whether it was my imagination, or whether he did try to abuse me.

With a lot of confusion and angst, the new setup was arranged, with my poor grandpa being kicked out of his own room and home – the one he'd built with his own two hands. He was living in a poor excuse of a room. We built a room downstairs in isolation for him, and he broke down. He became a skeleton of a man, not eating, losing his senses, and doing senile things like jumping naked into the mud in a trench in front of the house. He cried a lot and seemed so skinny. I wanted to help him. I wanted to speak to him, and I wanted my parents to try to help him, especially my dad. Soon my grandfather lost his mind and got angry at times. He no longer recognized me. He would beg and plead with me for food, for things I didn't understand. I would tell my mom. Most of the time, I think he was lost and lonely, and he just wanted someone to take care of him.

My mom told me not to talk to him, which made me feel even worse. He would extend his hands through the window and look at me with his gaunt face. His eyes were seemingly receding into his skull, and at these times, he seemed to look deep into my soul with accusation. It hurt. I think I will forever be haunted by images of my grandfather in the last stages of his life. What was I supposed to do? Sometimes I wish I'd had more guts and knew what to do when faced with situations.

My dad never saw the error of his ways, or if he did, he never made it known. He made all of us feel that we had to alienate my grandpa. I wish that I could go back in time and change the way my grandpa was treated in the last few years of his life. I know they say that elderly care is difficult, but we all get old one day. Even at that age – I was twelve years old when it got really bad – I knew it was wrong and wanted to fix it.

I became sad and angry, and I kept it bottled up. I became paranoid. I hated the neighbours too because they mean to my parents. I had denial going on full-blown, and I even became involved one day. I remember a light flashing in my head, and then I saw red. I started spouting angry words to the neighbour when my dad had started an argument. My parents were telling me to shut up. I think because all of my life I was silent, my sudden explosion may have scared them. This made them confused and angry with me, because they never quite understood how all my life experiences were adding up and affecting me. My years as a child were very confusing.

I grew to hate my neighbours, even the ones who were good to me, because my dad did not like these people. Out of loyalty to my parents, I succumbed to a bitter hatred for everyone who made my parents angry, whether they were right or wrong. Hatred is a nasty feeling, and if you carry this with you for years, it gives an acrid taste in your mouth and makes your head hurt. Your view of the world has blinders, thus narrowing your thoughts and channelling ugly feelings into your mind all the time. My dad even got angry when I would try to say hi; I was forbidden to have any contact with the two girls I used played with. It was so hard being told not to play, not to make friends. I really wanted to be one of these people. I was a child who wanted friends and needed to be able to play. The best times in the countryside were when I played with the children in the street and visited their yards and homes. In time I would outgrow my hate, but for years it became an internal blight and prevented me from enjoying what I should have found pleasure in.

I remember when the days were lighter and my days were brighter, and I did not need anything more than food and some quiet. Then I would read my books and relax in my imaginary worlds. My grandfather's yard had so many different fruit trees to eat from, and my friends had so many cool backyards to play in to create alternate worlds, but this all came to an end. This was when I was no longer allowed to play with the neighbouring children.

I knew at a certain stage that I became an introvert. I kept to myself not only at home but also at school. I made friends but found it hard to connect with them. I hardly spoke and internalized my thoughts. There were a few good friends who seemed to communicate with me and found me interesting enough to want to be my friend. I think I was ashamed of myself and my circumstances, and I was fearful of making friends. I felt safer within my space.

I found myself feeling a sense of surrealism at home. It was too hard to grasp, understand, and accept. My brothers got off easily (or harder) than me through total avoidance. They never were home; they only showed up to eat, bathe, and sleep. They never helped out at home, which is sad. My parents were overworked and of poor health, and they needed all the help they could get. I tried, and I felt good. If all bad things are happening at once, sometimes it gets too much for us, and then reality gets a little blurred. On order to survive, we live with a routine that gives us calm. This is what I did and will always do.

There were things in my life that I wanted to change, things I wished I had more control over. I wished that I could do more, make my mom smile, make her dress prettier, and get all the nice things in life. She deserved it because she was so good to me, and she did the best she could. I wished that I could take away all her tears, but as life would have it, this would not change for a long time, if ever.

My grandpa slowly but surely deteriorated, and he got senile and sick. It became a lot for my mom to take on. She had to bathe him, clean him if he messed himself, feed him, and get up during the nights when he cried. I vowed then that I will never look after an elderly person unless I was true to myself and knew that I could do it. I will never wanted to treat another old person the way my grandpa was treated. My mother did as much as she humanly could. Remember, this was the lady who kept the house clean, cooked three hot meals daily, did the laundry and dishes, made clothing, sewed into the wee hours of the night, and ran around to get her products sold quickly so she could then go grocery shopping. Now she had to do all these things for my grandfather. I tried to help, but she wanted me protected, so she would insist that I go read and iron my clothes.

I think I never got involved in saving or even trying to defend others because of my fear of my father. I did not want to recognize him as a bad person, but I think I realized that his emotions were unstable at an early age, so I tried my best to appease him. I really liked spending time with my grandpa, who was the best. I wanted to save my grandfather from my dad's wrath, but I was scared of Dad. I tried a few times and got so scared; I cannot even remember exactly what happened, but it must have been bad, because I stopped trying.

I remember all the years I spent with my grandparents during each summer break. Those were my best childhood memories. I remember my grandfather always taking me with him everywhere he went. I only have good memories of my grandfather. He loved me as much as a tough old guy could love a little girl, I will take it with me as a fond thought all my life. He took me to so many of his favourite places, and he always let me be a carefree child, free to run and play and not worry about anything. He made sure I was clean, ate, and went with him everywhere. I remember when he took me kite flying: he taught me how to hold the twine and run off to get the kite in the air. Then we would hold the ball of twine together, feeling the pull and tug of the kite.

My grandfather was so unlike my grandma, who seemed to resent me for some unknown reason. She never quite got too close to me. She did spend time with me and do girlie things with me, but she did not say much. I think this may be also because I looked very much like my dad, and she could not stand the sight of him. I wanted to be her favourite too. I wanted her to like me, but I think she was very unhappy and did not like too many people. I don't think my grandparents liked my father from the first day he entered my mother's life, and I don't think they ever accepted him over the years. I cannot say I blame them, my father was a difficult individual. If he liked you, you would sing his praises; if he didn't like you, you would hate him.

I have some funny and strange recollections of my grandpa. My grandpa was so strong that he would balance an axe on his forehead. I know it sounds crazy, but this was what he did to impress me and his friends. He could crush an anthill with his bare hands and not get bitten. His hands were hard from lots of outdoors living. He would make a slingshot and hit small birds, and then he would skin the bird, gut it, and bake it in the earth. I got to taste one, much to my parents' chagrin.

I wonder if my dad was jealous of my grandfather. Even though Grandpa was uneducated, he was rather handsome and strong. He bought lumber and made his house by himself. I think Dad often wondered how such an ignorant person like my grandfather could make his own house, have no debt, and be perfectly happy. Yet my father, with a fair amount of intellect and academic knowledge, was put into a situation where he had no choice but to live with and be obligated to my grandfather.

My dad did not accomplish much in terms of wealth. Looking back, I do believe that he made bad choices in life. He drank a lot when he was younger, and he spent a lot of his money partying with friends. He never saved or thought long-term. He was not a good example for my brothers; I don't think they ever stood a fair chance. When he got sick, and we became so poor we could not afford rent and were thrown on the streets by the landlord, where did we have to go? Nowhere but my grandfather's house. As I write, I think about how many emotions people can suppress until they are pressured to recall certain situations, and then it flows and hurts all over again.

My grandpa passed away in his nineties. I don't remember exactly how old he was, but he was old. Before the last few years of his life – before he deteriorated in front of my eyes and was treated badly – he lived happily doing what he wanted to do. I will always remember him as someone who lived well and did things for himself. I will grow up to be self-reliant like him.

I knew that when my grandpa passed away, a part of me and my life as I knew it ended. I felt older, and there was a new phase in my life. I became even more silent and read more. My hobbies were reading, listening to music, exercising (dancing to the radio, skipping), and doing housework. At this time, I was in my early teens and found that I was such a loner that I never knew what the other girls were talking about. I was such a nerd with limited knowledge of what went on in the teen years.

I didn't find the same things fun, and I didn't find it necessary to gossip or giggle. I found that growing up was really hard and not something I wanted. I thought that I was never going to fit into any of the circles in school. I never knew what to say and do. But that takes us to another phase, and I think I grew up a little.

CHAPTER 7

STILL GROWING

I went through a time of emptiness. I did things routinely. Life as a teenager was hard, and I never got to do any of the normal teenage things. I simply lived. I picked up exercising by looking at *Flashdance* and *Dirty Dancing*. I learnt that dancing was fun!

Smiling to myself, I would wait until both of my parents were out and then put on the radio. I'd dance my heart away, sometimes to near exhaustion, but it was fun. My dad somehow got it into his head that my brothers could run around aimlessly whenever and wherever, simply because they were boys. I could not, because as a girl my place was at home. I was supposed to be quiet and be married off when the time was right. When I danced, I gyrated and did whatever felt free. I rebelled through my music and exercises and let loose.

I also read even more books. I could have won a record for reading. I would flip through page after page, with time rushing by. I did the same things, tried to be content, and did whatever I could within the boundaries set. I learnt to keep peace. I have kept this throughout my life, and you will learn this as we go along.

I found that whilst dancing, I could put my imagination into a high gear and go to places in my head; this made dancing even more fun. I also listened to a lot of music when reading, and I would sometimes fall asleep and have dreams of a wonderful life free of money, where everyone was peaceful and happy. I would get a rush of adrenalin that would seem to lift me off my feet as the music pumped through my veins.

My constant need to be engaged in some form of activity kept me busy and physically fit. I swept the yard every day (it was all dust and dirt). I washed clothes and hung them out on clotheslines. I scrubbed the kitchen every week. I did whatever I could to stay busy and keep the house clean. I find dirty things make me uncomfortable and unhappy.

I read like there was no tomorrow. With nothing else to do, I read anything and everything, thirsty for knowledge. Rebellion set into my mind, but it was not premeditated, just natural growth. I think my resentment stemmed from not being able to live my life as a teenager. If there is one major regret I have had in my life, it is the time lost in the years that flew by, with me not having the chance to be a teenager. I was basically kept locked up in the house, away from life. I remember sitting on the veranda, and teenage boys would pass by. If they so much as looked at me, my dad came rushing out to usher me into the house. I developed a fearful approach to everything I did. I felt as if I had done something wrong, and when I went out, I carried that feeling with me. I was careful to not do anything that would upset my dad.

I was truly bereft of the fun my friends were having, and I may have developed a slower learning process. Emotionally and mentally I was immature, but I was in another world that my parents had created for me, and I became content or submissive.

I don't want to overanalyse. It got to the point where I felt that I never missed the other things my schoolmates were doing. I could not go further in school because my parents could not afford it, so for one year I passed by with housework, dancing, reading, sleeping, and relaxing. I flew through that year with no recognition of the fact that all my classmates were in disdain of me and did not understand why I was not still in school. Time went by, and things changed for people, but somehow I remained the same and felt as if I had missed an era.

I had no contact with anyone I went to school with, and no one seemed interested in me. I wrote letters to a few friends, my first boyfriend being one of them. I wrote to the boy who would enhance my life for years to come and make me alive in both good and bad ways. It was ironic. I was timid and had no self-confidence, but I could express myself freely when writing. I wrote letters as a way of reaching out to people I knew, so as to not drown in my world.

My father started talking about marrying me to people, like an arranged marriage. My world started looking even worse and scary. I felt that I was drowning into depths I could not pull myself out of, not by reading, dancing, or doing any of my other self-prescribed methods. My brother Brad was terrified and angry, and he put a stop to the conversation, thus protecting me and giving me the space to grow and fight for my freedom. I am so grateful for his intervention.

Sometimes while rocking in my hammock downstairs, I would look at the fruit trees and remember my grandpa taking me with him for those long walks to gather sand in big bags and bring them back to his garden. He took a lot of time growing his plants, nurturing and splicing. His mangoes were the best because they were a splice of two species; most of his fruit trees and plants were a combination. This was what had made him an awesome gardener.

The trees were sadly not the same anymore; it seemed as if they missed him too. The flowers lacked the radiance of bright colours, and I felt the same way. I felt guilty for not standing up for him and protecting him from my father. I resented my dad on so many levels.

I became angry and would break into sudden screaming bouts, shouting at everyone and hating my life, disliking the way we were living and the way our neighbours thought of us. I was ashamed of my life and my parents. My mom did not get it and thought I was being difficult. Can you understand the rage tearing on my insides? I never got to vent that horrid feeling into the winds. I kept it in, and it festered. I was an angry, quiet teenager who was well behaved, but eventually it gave way to outbursts of tears and screaming.

I had a lot of issues, I know. Most likely I still have a lot, but I am slowly working towards that Zen state of mind. I will always feel different from everyone because I think we all have our own memories and things we identify as forming us to be the way we are now.

I managed to keep the marriage process at bay, my brothers came to my rescue, and the topic became dormant. I felt a bit of reprieve for a bit and went back to what I did before. It was the same old things, but compared to marrying someone and changing my life completely, I was okay with it.

I developed routines and became a creature of habit – and also slightly anal. I remembered cleaning the house every weekend, scrubbing the floors on my hands and knees, and then making sure all books were aligned by size and colour. I'd blow up if my brothers so much as touched them. I would then shower, gather snacks (fruits from trees in huge bowls), grab a book, and immerse myself in my reading for the rest of the day. This pretty much took care of Saturdays and Sundays. Sometimes I went to church, and sometimes I'd go on a cleaning spree and sweep the entire yard. (Mind you, the yard was pretty much grass, dirt, and pebbles). Then I would sit in the hammock, daydreaming or reading the rest of the day.

Another note here, as my memory is jogged. Even my church attendance became an issue for my father, because I gained friends and went out with them to events at the church. Soon he also stopped my going to church.

It's funny how time flies: year after year, same thing. It all became an existence to me, and before I knew it, I was all grown up (theoretically). I was at the ripe old age of seventeen and knew it was time for me to try to fly the coop. I think I was smart enough not to do anything stupid like run away, and I waited until I could find a good reason for me to be able to easily leave the house. I had wanted so badly to start working because it became associated with liberty to me, and so it began when I turned seventeen.

CHAPTER 8

My Adult Life Starts

I started working at a bank at seventeen years old. I cannot remember the interview. I do remember who interviewed me and what was said to me. She was a fancily dressed woman who wore a lot of make-up and smiled, but she seemed aloof at the same time. I do not know what was said or how I replied, but somehow I got the job.

I remember getting dressed, being extremely sweaty and nervous, and thinking that the world was such a big and scary place. I didn't go out a lot on my own, and now I was being thrown into a totally different place. I was going to be away from home – a lot! That made me excited but a little scared at the same time; it meant I was out of the house, could go somewhere, and meet people every day!

I remember my first day at work. I was introduced to lots of people and eventually made it to the person whom I was taking over from. He was much older than I was, and he seemed so confident and sure about what he was doing. He introduced himself as Abdel, and over the next two days, I was trained to enter loan data and process data cards in a gigantic computer called Big Bertha. The rest is a blur. I was excited about working at the bank; it was an impressive-looking building, was new, and smelt great!

I do remember clearly sitting under a dripping air conditioning vent late in the evenings, wondering if this is what working was like. I did not complain because I'd never worked before, and really, a dripping air conditioner vent was nothing compared to growing up in a house that was always too hot or too windy at nights. So I rather enjoyed the cold air and dampness.

My dad was not too keen on the late nights I worked. Eventually, even work itself would become a bone of contention. My dad thought that working late for lots of nights and coming home in a taxi gave the neighbours wrong ideas. I was so innocent I did not understand, and somehow I felt culpable for something I would later realise was just my dad's way of controlling me.

Let's talk more about my home. My bed was stacked up high over my brother's double bunker, and at nights the wind came whistling through the spaces in the walls and through the broken windows and kitchen door. The kitchen door somehow was never fixed throughout all the years, and it made me have sleepless nights. The kitchen door was so badly damaged that even now, writing about it makes me cringe. I would have to lift parts of it to make it look as if it were a whole door from the outside, in the hopes that if a burglar came by, he wouldn't think it was falling apart and was easy to enter. I know – who in her right mind would even think about wanting to steal from a house that obviously contained nothing of value? But I didn't think of that; I went with my natural feeling of fear about everything. I think I was the only family member who got up several times in the nights to check if someone had come through the back door, and if I could magically seal it up.

The door was basically hanging by the hinges, and my family seemed incapable of fixing things; all they did was break things. I dreamt about the door and imagined fixing it. It was scary to live in a house where the doors and windows were falling apart. As for the front door, I would lock it tightly and bolt it, and when the wind blew, it would be wide open when I awoke! This should give you a better visual of just how broken my home was in more ways than one!

Let's go back to my work life. I went to work early every day, and it seemed like I opened the bank because everyone else came in much later. I got a head start on my job, which I knew nothing of, and wondered why in hell I had been given this job. But I was not someone to look a gift horse in the mouth, so I said nothing and merrily went about my way, learning and eventually doing a good job.

Everyone really liked me, and some were a little envious; I realized this after I was given a senior role and pay. I guess sometimes when people are quiet, we can assume they are either very smart or stupid, so most of the times I was mistaken for an intellect. I never felt like I quite belonged in this job; it was as if every day I talked to strangers. I did not bond with anyone, and I didn't have any friends who wanted to go to lunch with me. It was if I was in another realm, walking amongst people and still getting things done which connected to the real world. A tip to those out there who are not sure of yourself: keep quiet and listen, and everyone will think you are smart!

The bank itself was quite impressive from an architectural perspective, and it smelt good. There was a beautiful, handmade aquarium at the entrance of the foyer, and there were exotic fish and plants. The water also fell gently along a wall, simulating a waterfall. Inside the bank, it was pristine and very cold; everyone was smartly dressed, and the atmosphere was opulent.

Remember that this was my first job and my first attempt at independence.

I remember that there was a manager who wore rather short clothes and dressed fifteen years younger in a bid to quell the aging process. She was pretty, but this look did not complement her. I say this because she got mad when the younger girls wore short skirts, and she would write a warning memo or call them into her office, reading the proper dress code to them.

I remember quite a few people, and most were not friendly but were quite becoming in their appearance. I was in awe of them. I dressed simply and was not very fancy. My mom sewed my clothes, and they were pretty and fit me well, but they were definitely not expensive. I really was quite pretty and looked well dressed, but I would not come to know of this until much later in my life. I was so insecure, and because I was poor, I thought that everyone else was better than me. I never really looked at myself as someone others wanted to be.

After a few months of working really long hours, with the bitter cold dripping on me in the nights, my dad said I should think about leaving the job. I got scared and did not want to be home. I liked the experience of being away from home every day during the week and having money to buy groceries and occasionally treat myself. And the freedom! Yes, I know: going to work daily and going home straight from work does not fall into the freedom category for most of you, but remember what I started with!

I did agree with him that this was not good for me; it was pretty much not kosher to be arriving home late every night in a taxi from work. Neighbours were starting to yap about my coming and going. It was rather scandalous for a young girl to be out late in the nights, and I felt like I was doing something rather bad, so I agreed. I went about job hunting in a limited sense, and I sent my résumé to another bank, which was across from where I worked.

I got a letter for an interview within a few weeks, was hired the same day, and started working there the next week. I was just a few months away from becoming eighteen years old.

I remember sitting in the lobby and waiting on my first day at Bona Bank, with sunlight filtering through the overhead glass roof. I felt so happy and light-hearted, as if I knew I belonged. The building was not as impressive as the other bank, but somehow it was warmer and brighter. The people looked more down to earth, and everyone seemed happy. I sat next to a pretty girl with glasses who looked very quiet but not nervous. I didn't even realize that I looked even quieter, and I was quite surprised when she introduced herself. We started chatting and became the best of friends from that day. Her name was Andrea, and I had never met someone who was so genuine and smart. We bonded from that day, and I liked her a lot.

Then out came our outlandish manager of the bank. Man, she was ahead of the times, quite forceful, and full of energy. As for her clothes, she certainly had her own style. She greeted us both and complimented us on our abilities, regarding us as assets to her organization. To my inexperienced ears, this was worth far more than just words; I took her literally and felt special. I felt truly important!

It was my first day, and I wanted to learn everything and work really hard. I had this vigour and vim to give all I had and more, and I felt good about this bank.

As I said before, it was not as resplendent as the other bank; the foyer was simple and led right into the area for customers, with tellers in full view left and forward. The ceiling was very pretty: it was a dome, and the second floor was open concept and viewable from the ground floor. This gave the bank a welcoming and less uptight look than the other, which seemed (like most banks) like it was in lockdown after the ground floor.

I walked along with the hiring manager, who introduced me and Andrea to everyone. After walking around for more than five minutes, faces became a blur, and names were totally useless to me. Andrea also walked along and was introduced; she was pretty, polite, and friendly.

I am also outwardly friendly and polite, and I got looks from the guys as I slowly realized that I was pretty too. I am someone who loves being around people – but not being noticed. If attention is drawn to me, I become quite stupid and clumsy, and I exhibit poor social skills. I tend to become awkward and withdraw from interactions if they are prolonged. Then I would get the ugly complex, and I know that some of you can empathize with that feeling very well.

Much to my relief, the ordeal was not too long, and after introductions I was taken to the department, where I would start immediately. That made me feel very comfortable as I blended into the background and started filing invoices and ledgers. The papers sliding through my fingers provided comfort and reassurance to me that I really had started working and was being a contributor. Nobody paid too much attention to me, but they gave me guidance and work to do, which was right up my alley.

My second day at work was awesome, and so were the days afterwards. I got to leave home every day, and I wasn't questioned or treated as if I was doing something horrid whilst away! Ironically, I was the perfect teenager. I did my chores and then some, and I was neat and clean. I did not have a boyfriend. I did not smoke, drink, go out partying, or respond rudely to my parents. My parents were so set in their ways and were so afraid of me making mistakes that I was not allowed to make any – until much later, when I rebelled. As for accusations, I felt guilty even when I did absolutely nothing; it was the way they made me feel.

I earned money with my job. I'm not sure how much or where it went, because I spent it all on buying groceries for home and clothes for work. I gave my parents money if they asked. I know that they tried their best to do what was best for all of us, regardless of the way things were done, and it was done with good intentions. I went for walks during my lunch and slowly started to enjoy being at work and fitting in time for myself during the day, doing things that made me happy. I went to the museum, reminiscing about the days my mom would take me when I was smaller. I also went browsing for clothing and little trinkets.

I worked incessantly and hard, never minding the long hours because I had quite a few buddies who kept me company. We became really close friends, and we would laugh, sharing silly jokes and eating junk food. Sometimes we worked weekends, and I was usually the first person there. What a loser! But this was my happening time; to me, this made me feel happy and provided purpose, because there was nothing else to which I attributed myself.

My parents were not as concerned about my hours because they were not as late. Also, the first job must have made it easier for them to let go a little. Maybe I was also getting older and made more money, which helped them too. I was so busy and got caught up in working as my life. I never kept track of time and never complained, so I was promoted easily and went to another department, where the work was harder, the pay was better, and the friends were a bit different. These people were more mature and mean, and they thought it fun to poke fun at me. I took it in stride, because now I had a boyfriend, and I was constantly on cloud nine!

Here is the lowdown on how the boyfriend happened. I told you about that letter I wrote to an old school friend. One of the persons I had written a letter to was someone I knew from school. I had thought he was okay, but then after I left school, I saw him one day riding his bicycle, and my heart flip-flopped. He was super cute! His name was Jeremy, and he was tall, handsome, muscular, and refined. I had written to Jeremy when I had left school and never thought about it.

Years after, when I started working at the bank, my life changed. Jeremy turned up one day, ambling through my street. I was returning from work, and he was on his way out from my street, so we met halfway. It was surreal. He was better looking than I remembered him, and he was all grown up! He made me feel all fluttery inside, and to this day I cannot recall anything said. The sun was still shining brightly, and I had two large bottles of detergent in my hands. I remember the detergent because these things were heavy, and I was sweating and wondering why I'd done this to myself. But when I saw Jeremy, and suddenly the bottles were weightless! My heart stopped, and I smiled. I must have been coherent because he spoke back, and there was this instant of a really solid connection that made breathing difficult and seeing rather strange. Also, there was a feeling that we were alone, even though we were standing in the middle of the road with people walking by and staring.

From that day, I became alive. It was whirlwind dating, and we started going out the same day. He came by later in the evening. I told my dad a friend was coming to get me, and Jeremy had to answer many questions. It seemed my dad knew his dad, so it was okay with him. We went for bike rides and strolls, and we spent all our spare time together. I don't think I paid much heed to my parents' warnings, which came as time went by, that I was moving too fast and seeing too much of

Jeremy. They also thought he was too rich for me and would never marry me. Their words fell on deaf ears.

I had taken Jeremy to one of the bank's staff outing, and we danced and chatted – or rather, he chatted. I was a mess because I knew that we would eventually kiss; that was what all the movies said happens after a few dates, right? I wanted to but didn't know how to, and I was so weirded out about it that I started giggling.

I was kissed for the first time at eighteen, and I kept my eyes closed, waiting for stars and lights to explode – but I got slobbered on! I did not know what to do with my mouth or tongue. It was too funny: I truly expected lights and flashes, and thinking about it still make me smile. Jeremy did not seem to know what to do with his tongue and lips either, which is why I got slobbered upon. It was quite a funny experience, and I wanted to giggle incessantly, but after a while I found my shyness and was quiet. I was happy that this hunk was interested in little old me, with the poor childhood and all that. Funny how some of us wear our experiences and circumstances either as a shield or as an inferiority exterior. I was the latter.

All of my life before Jeremy, I felt insignificant and never felt proud of myself or liked myself. I felt less than almost everyone. I say almost because regardless of how dire your situation is, there is always someone else who is worse off. Jeremy made me feel beautiful and sexy and full of life, and I wanted to express all of this to him. With time, slobbers turned into heated moments, precious time spent together, feelings so incredibly exhilarating and bursting with energy. I cannot adequately describe my feelings. I never quite knew what to say out loud, so for me, my relationship was rather quiet for many years, but I was emotional and very much in love. I gave my heart and soul to my boyfriend, never thinking where we would end up or if I would get hurt.

My parents were quite concerned and never wanted me to date. First, it was not the proper thing to do because the neighbours would talk. After that, the list became long: he was rich, he was too good-looking, he was using me. My father worried about me becoming a marked person. I would continue, but you see, some things never quite go away, and the hurt remains. My parents were protecting me in their own way, but along they were hurting me more than anything. So I forgive them, knowing that their intention was good and their love made them blind. To explain what a marked person is, it's someone who is female, has sex before marriage, and is then dumped, as if she's used up, is cast away, and is no good for anyone else (according to my parents' beliefs).

I continued merrily along my way with Jeremy because when I was him, nothing else mattered. Not my parents nagging at me, not work. All the time we spent together was my paradise and made me forget that what I'd experienced before was despair. For me, it was like a light shining on me and making me see the world through a different lens. I became popular, and I suddenly knew where all my friends were, the people with whom I'd gone to school. Yes, I forgot that I had a few friends at school. I would bump into them when Jeremy and I went on dates. All the boys who had crushes on me at school seemed to surface, and I felt good about myself. Being with Jeremy made me start living and seeing the rest of the world with all my old schoolmates. I realized just how shut off I had been. I felt so popular and attractive!

I was introduced to socializing, dancing at clubs, sitting on the sea walls with popular people, hanging out together, and being noticed. Everyone seemed to want to be my friend; guys wanted to date me because they knew I was dating Jeremy, and so this made me more attractive. I hung out with all the cool people and changed a lot during this time. This was my journey to adulthood, working and getting a boyfriend, and I thought this made me quite the adult! I had so much more to learn and experience, and I had only touched the surface of growing up.

Jeremy was very handsome, and most of the girls at the bank envied me, though I was unaware. I was so stupid that I thought if I never did anything to hurt anyone, the whole world would be my friend. In time, I would change. My heart has always been open and kind, and the way I think and treat others has been kind. I was so naïve that I never tried to analyse people's ulterior motives or suspect them of any negativity. My life would change, and so would I as time went by.

CHAPTER 9

ADULT LIFE CONTINUES

I got pregnant when I was almost nineteen, and I was so scared. I knew I could never let my parents know. I ate breakfast and was about to go to work when I got seriously nauseous and threw up everything. My mom was around but didn't say anything; she simply helped me. I think she knew and wanted to say something, but I had put a wall around me like most teenagers do. It was a defence mechanism. Also I think she didn't know how to deal with it, so she went with denial and hoped for the best.

I told Jeremy, who got worried. Only then did I accept the fact that I was pregnant. I was truly inexperienced in every way; never having had sex with anyone prior to Jeremy, I had no clue as to what to do next. I had illusions of life and thought that having unprotected sex was somehow all right, and that Jeremy took care of everything so nothing like this would happen to me. Well, I was wrong. I went to work and became so sick all day long that I couldn't do anything. I went home and pretended that nothing was out of sorts when my mom was around.

I had a flashback to when I was much younger and got my period. I remember the day so clearly. I was standing and looked down to see blood flowing down my legs. I did not get any pains and symptoms to indicate anything was happening to my body. I never even spoke about my periods with my mom; I remembered looking down at the floor when I first bled and thinking, *I am dying? What happened?* I was so frightened that I went to my mom and never said anything. I just showed her the floor, and she said, "That's part of growing up." And that was it. Then came the physical body changes and the bra. It was so blasé, with no big conversation. My mom avoided explaining anything about life because it made her uncomfortable, and maybe that is the way she was brought up. Life happens to everyone, and I think she went through the similar experience with her mom, so she felt there was no explanation needed.

Even though I read a lot, it was not associated with the real world, this was my alternate, so anything that was logical or I could have deduced became rather foggy until I could not get away from the reality anymore. Hence, what follows after I realized I became pregnant may seem disconcerting and stupid to some, but others may empathize.

Jeremy knew a doctor who did abortions. I went with him, but I never knew where we were going and what I was going to have to go through. We never even discussed it – he made the decision, and I silently went with him. I was too scared and wanted everything to go back the way it was before: all happy and spending my time with Jeremy with no other concern in the world. To this day, I am sure we never said, "Hey, we are going to a doctor, and this is what will happen." We did not discuss anything. I remember everything so clearly about this time in my life.

We sat amongst strangers and felt like strangers ourselves, sitting apart. The doctor came out, met with Jeremy, asked him what he was doing there, and told him to wait outside in his car. The doctor would take care of it. Jeremy's family was very wealthy and well-known in the community, and the doctor knew who he was and was friends with his dad. He did not want him to be seen in his clinic for anyone to get word back to his family or social circle. No, Jeremy would not be affected or tainted by this incident.

I went in alone, drank tablets, stripped, and was annihilated. I felt my insides being torn apart and vacuumed out. After what seemed like an eternity of being sucked empty, I groggily looked at the nurse, who told me I needed to get up. I did, and she gave me an extra-large pad. I put it on and got dressed. I sat there in an absent state of mind for not very long before the nurse came in and told me to leave. I barely had time to sit up and feel as if I was still alive; I was in shock as I left. What had happened to me, and why did I do it?

I wanted to cry, but I didn't know how to. I felt so confused and bewildered. I went to the front and was told to collect a prescription with tablets. These were contraceptives, something I didn't know about. I guess it was common for this to happen to others; it seemed like a routine practiced by the clinic. This was how I learned about birth control.

As I walked out, I noticed Jeremy sitting in his car. His head was down, and he didn't ask me anything. It was a quiet ride to his brother's house, where I had no choice but to rest because I was bleeding profusely and was so drugged up. I fell asleep for the rest of the day and awoke startled and lost. Jeremy came in after a while and asked me if I wanted to eat or drink anything. Jeremy was very caring and loving, yet cruel and distant when he felt pressured. I felt so bereft that I did not know what to do, and I rested a bit more. Then I realized that it was around the time I would return home from work. so I went home.

My world was shattered, and my life changed from that day; I simply didn't know it. My self-esteem fell through the floor, and I somehow became more dependent on Jeremy. Instead of resenting him, I felt as if this was my fault, and I had to make it up to him before I lost him. I do not think as my life continued that I ever took time along the way to acknowledge major life-changing events and identify emotions. I kept everything to myself until many years later. I never acknowledged at this time of my life that I was not in this alone, that everything I went through should have been a shared experience, and that I needed his support more than anything. We needed to speak about this and be open with each other.

In my quest to please Jeremy and keep him happy, I engaged in detachment from my bodily concerns and pains, and I appeared normal and happy. I merrily went along in my relationship, in total denial of the recent happenings. I soon got pregnant again because I didn't take my birth control pills regularly. I know, you are thinking I was irresponsible, and I admit I was. At this time, I had tried to wash away my first abortion, and I had been living under this pretence that everything was good and that the first time had never happened. I was totally numb and knew for sure that I was pregnant again. I knew what would happen, and everything came rushing back to me. All the memories floated to my throat, making me gag and my head swim in pain. Was I scared? Yes. Was I stupid? Yes. Did I feel bad or think perhaps that maybe I could keep the baby, and Jeremy and I would get married and live happily ever after? I wanted to think there was a glimmer of hope left in me, and I still wanted to live happily ever after. I really wanted him to say this time that he was sorry for the first time, and that he loved me and wanted to marry me so we could raise this baby together.

But this time, Jeremy wanted no part in accompanying me or even discussing the fact that I was pregnant. He totally put it off until he knew he had to go on a trip with his family, and he told me to look after it. I didn't know what to do and who to turn to. I felt so lost and wanted to talk to my mom, but she didn't suspect anything this time, and it was too difficult for me to open up to her. I didn't know who to turn to, and I knew then I had to go through this again. However, this time I was truly alone. Would I be able to pretend and carry on this time? I felt so sad and broken. I knew that this made life a reality, and I was not living in a fairy tale romance. I could not believe that Jeremy wanted me to go by myself and had left the decision to me. I would learn that was his mode of operation, to step away from life's realities. All must be well and sex was great, but no consequences were to be placed in his corner. It was easier for him to step away and enjoy the benefits of the relationship without the pain. Who was I fooling? I think he simply wanted sex. He was a nice guy but changed as he got older. He was very handsome, so with other women ogling him, I knew that he was thinking of expanding his horizons and experiences. His mom also didn't want him to be involved with me because she didn't think I was good enough for him.

I went alone and did everything, and to this day, I do not remember anything. Or rather, it blurred with my first time, and I think I was given more anaesthesia. This time around, I think I was too messed up and went through the motions of the abortion without trying to feel anything. I kept my mind blank so I wouldn't remember anything, or maybe it just hurt too much to keep all that repressed all the bloody time!

I was really drugged this time, and afterwards, it felt like a total memory lapse. What I do remember is walking away, not quite steadily, from the clinic with heavy feet and a heart like lead, tears brimming in my eyes. I remember walking along the sidewalk. A few guys looked at me appreciatively, and I thought, *Can you not see my pain, my blood, my broken heart and body?* I wanted to scream this out but didn't. I felt that anyone looking at me would see what I did and how I felt.

I remember going home on a crowded, sweaty bus with loud music blaring on the cheap speakers. I was happy that no one looked at me. I remember getting home, locking myself in my room, and crying nonstop. I remember becoming angrier each day, and as time passed, I stopped noticing my personality changes. I think this was the stage where I started storing up all my feelings to the point where I would react to Jeremy instead of being quiet and submissive.

Sometimes when life's moments stun us, we survive better by numbing ourselves. For me, I was stupid and thought my world revolved around my boyfriend; everyone else was a nuisance and wrong, and he was the only good and right thing in my life. I did not try to reach out to my parents and instead shut them out. I became ashamed of who I was and of my family. I started to reach outside my home, to become someone else. I wanted to move away and start a new life, and I dreamt of living anywhere else but at home.

I stayed in this relationship for many years, mainly because I did not know anything else and also because I could not get out of my house any other way. My father forbade me from going out unless it was with Jeremy. I was also still foolishly in love with Jeremy, and he made my heart beat profusely every time I saw him. My world still lit up because I never admitted that after all that had happened, my old self was dying. You will see after my relationship that all the fruits became sour grapes, and I would be an idiot even more.

It is ironic that instead of having three children who never messed up in life, my dad got three with screwed-up minds and lives. My dad was so adamant about discipline that all of his children got really messed up. It was the opposite of everything he wanted. But even if I tried, I never quite understood why he was the way he was. I tried to understand and empathize with his circumstances – loss of chances at a better life, no money, bad health, unhappy in his marriage – but still, we were his children. Why did he think it was perfectly fine to hit his sons? Why did he think beating them senseless would make them better, make them respect him and love him? Why did he think controlling me through fear would keep me under control?

My brothers hated my father. I hated him too, but as I got older, it became more of a tolerance. Can I say I loved my dad? It's not easy to answer; it will have to remain unanswered. I realized he did what he thought was best for us, and he loved us in his way. I am grateful to him for his teachings and most of what he has said; it did have more than an inkling of truth in it. I cannot blame my parents for any of my circumstances, so if it comes across that way, remember that as adults we choose who we are with, what we do, and when we do it. My parents did what they felt was best.

My circumstances may have been better if I was allowed the chance to grow, to be with my friends and not feel fearful and trapped in a house filled with yelling and abuse. There is so much anger filling my heart, and it brings back memories that were pushed under. I may never have felt the need to have a boyfriend, and maybe I would have walked away from Jeremy when the first signs of a bad relationship surfaced. Who knows? I know deep in my heart, I am still to be held accountable for all my actions. People have grown up in much worse situations and have turned out splendidly.

Lying in my bed, I tried to think of what I would do with my life. I was now twenty years old, and when thinking of my job, I wanted more. I was not sure what more I wanted, but I knew that my life had to have more of something. I felt that I had lost a major part of my soul, and I wanted to regain it. I wanted to see the world as I had before reality set in. I knew I was unhappy with Jeremy, but I focused on everything but the source. I simply could not stand the idea of my life without him.

CHAPTER 10

REALITY BITES

I stayed with Jeremy for a long time. I never questioned the future because then I would have to acknowledge the truth. I was truly without direction and had lost all my ambition and drive to achieve. I also hopelessly loved him and could not think of my life without him. Strangely, I never thought of being married and growing old with him; I simply never thought of a life without him, with no defined future. I knew this would never happen, but a drowning man grasps at straws.

I guess if you stay in a situation where you are valued at less than what you are worth, eventually it breaks you and makes you into that image. I became an insipid little fool in love and was totally incoherent about doing things to complete me and to make me grow as an individual. Over the years with Jeremy, my growth as a person was stunted, locked in a young girl's dreams of life with a lover.

I became totally dependent on Jeremy for attention, love, freedom to step out of my parents' home, and sex. Was the sex good? It was, but again, what did I have to compare it with? In retrospect, it was like many first relationships wherein the woman is submissive because of ignorance and trust. The man is dominant and self-assured, confident that the woman is his and will not need to be maintained with compliments or much affection. Basically, the relationship became one of comfort and reliance. We did have passion, and my heart did flutter – but had I known someone else who was more caring and attentive, more genuinely in love with me, what would I have to say then? This was when things got worse, and we started drifting apart rather drastically.

I remember going out with Jeremy to a bar. The night was pretty, and I looked pretty – at least, I thought I did. Guys looked in my direction, and I enjoyed dancing, so this was fun! I danced my heart away and felt on top of the world, until I saw Jeremy glancing over to a very sexy brunette in the far corner of the club. She sashayed in rhythm to the music, provocatively swaying her hips, and he kept his eyes locked on her. I could feel the chemistry, and suddenly I felt ugly and insignificant. It was as if I was not even inside the club with him, and I felt so small. I realized how inexperienced and gauche I was when I felt that girl's confidence oozing across the room. I felt all my flaws.

I wanted so badly to run, and I was relieved when Jeremy asked me if I wanted to go home. I did, and he dropped me off quite in a rush. My guess was that he went back to the club. My guess proved to be accurate, as I learned soon. This girl would become his next girlfriend, a notch on his belt, and he would prove to have a very long belt with multiple notches!

I remember being at his home and hanging out a lot – perhaps too much. A girl with whom I noticed he sometimes hung around called him one day while I was lazing by his home. He grabbed the phone and ran off into his room, closing the door behind him. My blood rushed to my head and ears, and my heart was pounding. I rushed after him, jealousy tearing away my insides. I acted rather stupidly, yelling and screaming until he hung up. Our path went downhill fast. I blamed myself for being insecure and thought I'd overreacted. Jeremy was not really doing anything wrong … was he? He was, and he became a sleazeball, cheating in every which way. I still could not fall out of love – what is that sickness, anyhow? Why do we go through stages in our lives when we allow people to treat us badly?

After all these years, I have done an audit on my past behaviour. With some analysis, I realize that I am a very intense individual. Not too many people are like that, especially those young men looking to have it all without giving up anything. I know I sound bitter and should not generalize, but seriously? The truth is most young women would have done exactly what I did. The only thing is, I felt remorse and felt that I owed *him* an apology, cutting my self-esteem even further. We all think that something is wrong with us if our other half seems superior in looks and prestige, and is adored by others.

How many of you can lay claim to having a boyfriend whom you went out with for more than eight years, and who is faithful to you and truly loves and adores you? And who has lifelong plans with you? Probably quite a few. I was a foolish young girl, truly ignorant of the world, so bear with me as I transgress down this path of stupidity and love. My folly does not predict the folly of others, but it does provide something interesting to describe.

I awoke one day and felt really alive. I looked out the window and felt eager at the thought that today I would see Jeremy. I did not. He called and said that we should break up. He said he needed space to grow, and so we needed to be apart and grow up. In other words, he started seeing that girl from the club and wanted to be with her. I saw them that very same day as I went for a walk. He did not waste any time! Now I will let you into my world of pain experienced at this bitter stab of reality and lost love.

From reading a lot, I knew expressions like "cuts like a knife" and "piercing pain to the heart". I figured it was not quite physical. Man, was I wrong! It fucking hurt. I doubled over in pain and cried, and when I thought I could not cry anymore, tears still flowed. The pain was indescribable. I thought I was dying a slow death: my breath was in hitches, my stomach was a mess, my insides had a war of feelings, my head was disconnected from my body, and my eyes hurt! I could not stop crying, and tears flowed endlessly. I could not stop the insurmountable pain. I felt like there was a never-ending well of water flowing through my eyes, and I felt raw and torn inside.

I did not know what to do and had no one to talk to. My mom heard me keening, and I yelled through my angst for her to stay away. She wanted to help me, to be there for me; I know that now. When I told her to leave me alone, I hurt her too. I never stopped to think of my mom, and I would not realize it until much later in my life how much I'd pushed her away. I complained of never being close to her, but maybe I also never tried. I thought I was better than her – the folly of youth. I thought I knew more because I was educated and she was not. I can never become the calibre of woman my mother is. She is strong, valiant, and loving, and she will always love me despite my faults.

I went to sleep. Days became a blur, and then weeks and months went by with me sitting at home, my life at a standstill. My dad calling me a marred woman, and I accepted it. I had no confidence, was truly broken, and was a fucked-up mess. I found everything to be lacking: my life, my body, my mind, my job, my friends, my family, even the people who lived in my neighbourhood. I became paranoid because I thought I was worth nothing and it was my fault. I was so depressed that you could have told me anything, and I would have believed it to be true. I was lost and broken.

I recall Jeremy's mom taking me aside a month before our break-up and having a serious chat with me. I do believe she encouraged him strongly in his quest to gain his experiences. She saw that we were really close and wanted the best for her son. To her, I was not the best not by a long shot. She wanted to let me know that she thought I was a wonderful person; however, we were both too young to be so serious, and she thought we should see other people. She said if I loved Jeremy, I would give him his space, and if he loved me, like a butterfly he would fly back into my life. I did not take her seriously at that time and thought she was giving me advice as a caring person. I will always remember the butterfly comment, because it makes me smile sadly even now. I think about how naïve I must have appeared.

I became less sad, and little by little I changed to a bitter, embattled person. I lashed out at my parents and brothers, kept to myself, went to work, exercised furiously, read, listened to music, and cried myself to sleep every night. Yes, I was an angry person, so I also became desperate. I was in a really low place, and the darkness enveloped me as only depression can.

Then Jeremy called, and I became a person in denial. My heart jumped with joy, and I read between his words. I convinced myself that he still cared about me and was telling me that he missed me. He must have felt guilty and wanted to see if I was okay. This was what my brain told me.

Feeling excited and lost in a fool's world, later that day I got dressed and went by his house. My mom told me not to go, and I lied, saying that I was just going for a walk. When I got there, Jeremy was exercising. I found him so fucking hot that I didn't say anything when he started kissing me. We ended up having sex, and it was good. He sat with me for a bit and told me that this did not change things; we were still not together because he was with someone else. He never resisted kissing me, or having sex, but he seemed very firm about this being just a screw. Man, I really was stupid. Time after time I would be treated rather badly, and still I went back for more! He then dropped me off at home. I was happy with the paltry crumbs he threw my way but felt a little numb. I felt stupid, but somehow this still provided hope that we would make up and get back together, because what we had was irreplaceable. My smart side told me what a piece of work he was and what a mess I was to even think of him as someone who is good, but that voice was small and dying.

Love makes us all do things we would never ever dream of, and sometimes we do things we would berate ourselves for after. But truth be told, we fall in love again and again, and we do the same shit over and over. Until we become jaded, and then it's too late. Time went by, and I did not keep track of reality, only significant events that involved Jeremy.

Jeremy came back into my life, and I let him, even though my father was upset. Jeremy told my dad that he was serious about me and had plans to marry me. He had gone by my dad's workplace to persuade him to let him see me again. My dad told me this, and I asked for it. After a year of changed feelings, I was now more guarded and less emotional. I found that I was with Jeremy more so to protect myself from public hanging. Like my dad, I felt that I was marred, and as such I was better off with Jeremy than without. What a sad way to think. Jeremy had broken up with that girl from the club – but that was not the last. He was on the way to becoming a serial cheater. I felt that no one else wanted me, and so I may as well be with the one person who'd have me, even though he made me feel lesser. I was an addict for Jeremy when it came to sex. I could not resist him, and the physical attraction was overwhelming.

We continued, but I knew that my boyfriend was straying. He wanted more notches in his belt, and ... I heard about him from others. Some of my girlfriends decided I would be better off knowing all the dirty details. And so the ride downhill began again. I don't remember much here; I simply remember the years going by with constant hurt and depression. I kept going out with him, giving myself no credit, with no time for friends, just Jeremy. My parents were almost invisible and of no importance. My world revolved around Jeremy.

Chapter 11

Eyes Open

Sometimes things happen for a reason. I kept this mantra in my head every time bad things happened to me, because it kept me sane and made me think of even the worse possible scenario as a temporary state. Imagine if we could all surpass the feeling of helplessness and feel empowered, even when caught in the most hurtful state. We could think of the afterwards during whatever we are experiencing, and we'd know with some certainty that it would either be worse or better, but chances are it would end somehow.

I tried thinking outside of the box. That makes you see yourself from other eyes – the eyes of those watching you, the people who may be concerned (or appear concerned). I know this seems all negative, but it's really not. Empathy works for most of us; we simply do not know how to fit into shoes other than our own, but it can work. Then the world would be so much better. Sometimes I wonder about that statement. How does the world become a better place if we were all nice and kind? Would that mean then we would somehow find something else that makes others fall out of society's boundaries? My mind became one of confusion and was embattled with thoughts endlessly floating through. When we are lost, we truly are lost in our thoughts and feelings, and the world becomes a separate reality from our day-to-day existence.

So, back to my wonderful first love and boyfriend, who treated me like shit and expected me to accept it. I was deemed somewhat lower than his class and should have been grateful to be his girlfriend. I know it's because his mom told him and his brother that it was not unusual to date lots of girls at the same time, having no real commitment. His mom and brother both were nice to me, but I know that they did not think I was good enough for Jeremy. One of my girlfriends told me this; she was close to his mom, who had confided that she was glad that we were not together anymore. His mom was worried about Jeremy marrying outside of his class. I know her motive for telling me was not necessary out of the goodness of her heart; it was more so malicious information in order to see me suffer. I realized later she was not my friend and also thought I was inferior to her.

I practically lived with Jeremy, and I spent all my days at his house. I even slept over on weekends. I remember on a sunny and bright day, I had fallen asleep and awoke to voices. I went out on the veranda, where I saw him talking to a girl who was infatuated with him. He was chatting with this younger girl, and after having been with him for more than six years, I felt old. I was a very insecure and jealous person! I blew a fuse and made such a ruckus. I embarrassed myself and didn't care. This is what happens when you fall in love and become so besotted: you lose all your marbles, and your brain cells get fried. It was so stupid!

Sometimes we get caught in situations where we think we have no escape, or rather, we have become so accustomed to what we are experiencing that this seems normal. And why fight against normal? I tried to fight for what was lost, and even knowing this, or maybe especially knowing this, made me into this desperate creature, someone with extremely low self-esteem. I cried and never quite spoke up, and I was so happy for any attention given to me, clinging to it with the last vestige of hope and thinking, *Oh, well, he's not with those girls – he's with me.* This was one of the events where his mom told me that I should leave him alone. He was not doing anything wrong.

This was why I sometimes felt lost. Why did my mother never speak to me about life as it was? I find it so hard to deal with life, not quite grasping the complexities (or lack thereof) of other people's thoughts. I felt somehow as if I was really stupid and different from everyone. I felt broken. Something had changed, and somehow we broke up again for good this time.

We didn't end with words, just absence. He never had the courage to speak his thoughts, and he never was big enough to own up to his mistakes. Somehow, I don't think he ever will. But for me, I was free. Though not knowing my freedom and not accepting my reality, instead living with my sad and lonely thoughts, delayed my freedom.

Various events had to take place before I could get out of my sinkhole. My dad berated me, blamed me for my sad state of affairs, and called me a fallen woman, someone no one would ever want. He made me feel besmirched and even smaller than I had felt with Jeremy. It was a vicious cycle to be in: used emotionally, broken, torn apart by my dad, made to feel even smaller time and again during my relationship with Jeremy. I would get out of this and would be a better person for my experiences. I guess in my dad's disappointment with me, this was his best defence and way of coping with my situation. My dad had high aspirations for me and wanted me to become the best I could, somebody with a great future and career. I understand this now, but it doesn't lessen the pain I felt then.

Sometimes as parents, we say things without abandon, and we spend most of our lives regretting the words and effects. I thought my dad was a loving person but was somehow misguided in his parenting skills. I do not blame him for any of my mistakes made along my less than merry path of life. My dad was from a different generation and was brought up to think along narrow passageways. So ended the era of Jeremy – finally!

CHAPTER 12

After the Break-up

B ona Bank no longer seemed so interesting to me. By then the years had flown by, and I was into my early twenties. So much of my life from eighteen to twenty-three was a blur: images of sex, internal conversations, bike rides, late nights, and work at the bank – they all seemed like a flow of constant events.

I got promoted. Work was an elixir; I engrossed myself in different tasks, and time flew by. Day in and day out, it was the same routine, mixed in with some walks. I find even now that walking is my way of resolving all internal battles and clearing my mind of dark and heavy emotions.

My new role was a great opportunity. In retrospect, it was probably a curve in career paths for me, and I think I became stupid and screwed up during and after my relationship with Jeremy. I was never quite was the same for almost eight years, took life as is, and never questioned my circumstances or analysed options. Thus came about a real spiral of events for the next few years.

I awoke one morning and thought of my life at the bank. I thought of my friends, who were never my friends but kept close to me so they could be close to Jeremy. I had mentioned before that he was a looker, and he had the female gender salivating whenever they saw him. He wore painted-on jeans and was tall, muscular, and handsome in a rough way. Yet he was genteel in speech and was such a smooth talker that he could talk the panties off women.

As you can tell, I was still in love with him after our break-up. He had the ability to make my stomach queasy and my heart feel heavy, with my blood pounding rapidly and my breath quickening. I also could not think clearly whenever I saw him. I tell you that I started a new life, yet it was still attached to the one person who'd made a mess of it. I got promoted and was still so psychologically screwed up that I could not function properly. But because I was in denial and figured I was over him, I thought that it was the job that provided no happiness. So I made such a shit-ass decision: I stuck with it for one year and then quit. Yep, I quit with no other job to go to. What a thing to do, with my parents having no money whatsoever! Now I was stuck at home with my parents, relentlessly berating me for not working, not being married, and not being a good person. What a screw-up!

I knew I needed a new, clean break from everything that made me despondent, so I quit my job at the bank. I became even more withdrawn because I was now without a job, had nowhere to go, and had no money. I became paranoid and felt that I needed an out, so I looked for work. Finally after a few months of climbing the walls at home, I found a decent job. It paid very little and was a step down from my job at the bank, but the company was reputable and the work not so bad.

The funny thing was, I enjoyed my work there; I simply never had enough money to go to any fun activities. I made enough money to buy groceries and gave them to my parents, and I also bought things for the house. I felt like I saw life differently. I now had freedom to choose what I wanted to do, and my life no longer revolved around Jeremy.

I made some new friends, and they were people I normally would have not made friends with because I was pretty judgemental in my youth. My new friends were poor like me, grew up tough, and were very down-to-earth. My work was very brainless – lots of money counting, paperwork, and routine tasks – but my co-workers were fun. They were younger and full of life, and boy, were they crazy! I usually gravitated to rich and better looking people, which did not make me very smart, did it? There was hope I would change in time.

Patty, Gayle, Tim, Annette, and Mavis made me feel liked and wanted, and they also made me take a look at my life again. I saw a young woman, with so much on her side who was not using it but going downhill – and not trying to fight it. I saw that my life did not need a huge salary and a boyfriend. I realized at this stage in my life that I could do anything I wanted, and do it really well.

I stayed at this job for a few months. My dad was not willing to accept that this was all I would be doing for the rest of my life, so he applied to jobs for me. I think even though you may feel I hate my dad by now, I do not. He was instrumental in making me who I am, driven and always wanting more, because he knew I could do it.

During my time there, I dated a co-worker for one week. Nothing happened, and he was a poor substitute for a boyfriend. Yikes – judgemental again. It was true, though. He was not smart, not kind, dishonest, and unattractive – and he already had a girlfriend. I was using him to get over Jeremy, my first attempt to wipe away my memories. Poor guy. I guess he was happy when I left that job.

In the meantime, Jeremy could not stay away from me. This begs me to ask the question: Why is it when we women don't want men, then they want us? He came by my workplace a lot to take me for lunch and to meet me in the afternoons, yet he did not want to make up. He simply wanted to make sure I was doing well, and to check that I did not have anyone else in my life. What a jerk!

When we women are begging and giving all we got, you guys are not interested. Then when we hit that brick wall, have optimized our emotions, have nothing left and want no more, you want us. Why is this?

When he came by my workplace, he made my new co-workers crazy with lust. They told me so! The girls thought he was handsome and couldn't understand why I was not dating him. Maybe they did not believe it and thought I was lying. I did not try to see him after work, and I accepted his visits as a friend but did not look for more. I wanted to see if there was life out there for me, with or without someone else.

I went for lots of walks and started feeling pretty, alive, and young again. I wanted to smile at people, heard birds in the trees, and felt the sun shining on my skin. I saw a cute guy a few times when I went for walks during my lunch, and he came up to me to chat. He was interested and wanted to start seeing me. I was hesitant but wanted to try. I started dating him very innocently. I would meet Trevor at the back of the building after work, and he would walk with me on my way to get a cab home. I would talk to Trevor for a long time until it got late and I had no choice but to go home. Then eventually I would take my cab home.

I tried going to the movies with him, but after my failed first relationship, my dad prevented me from going anywhere with anyone, even with my few girlfriends, so I was trapped between work and a few hours here and there to meet Trevor.

I think my dad should have let me live my life; maybe then I would not have had to keep trying to break free and make many more mistakes. Because of my lack of freedom, I felt I had to grab whatever chances I had with someone, instead of being able to think and select carefully because I had choices.

I really wanted to date this guy. He was extremely handsome and likable, and he wanted to hang out with me. We chatted for hours when we met. Eventually, because I could not get out to date him, he gave up, but we kept in contact via phone. I had no new relationships and was back to square one, with no freedom but at my workplace. However, I did not feel the urgency to get out there as much, and I started going back to my old self with compliancy because I felt I would again disappoint my parents. It was just too much of a struggle to get my freedom. Besides, I was very afraid of going against my parents because I felt that losing Jeremy was my fault.

I took the time to think about my life and tried to start a new one. At this job, I made no silly mistakes. It was just me being myself, enjoying being with friends, and overcoming my first real relationship.

CHAPTER 13

New Job and New Person

M y dad sent an application to an airline for a cabin attendant role. I had no idea what this was. My limited exposure beyond banking and working at my current job in a cambio (foreign exchange counter) kept me in certain boundaries, so this was all new for me. I was ridiculously immature for my age and did not know much beyond what I had experienced. Soon my world would change dramatically, and I would fly free!

I had visions of a cabin like on a ship, but in the air and doing who knew what – washing dishes and cooking? Go ahead and laugh; it's okay, I'm good with that. I laugh at my silliness too, except for my stupidity, which is a different story altogether. It is really funny when I look back at some of the things I misinterpreted and the things I did. It is actually quite hilarious. And no, I am not talking about my "mistakes"!

The weeks flew by after my dad applied for this job, and I did not think much about it. Then I got a letter from the airlines, asking me to come in for an interview, and seemingly my life opened up. Life became bigger, and the world became my oyster – not a place where I was insignificant and had no choices, but one in which I could literally soar with the birds. I became free! I started feeling important. It was so weird. I never got the time to think about anything because it all happened so fast! I did not think anything would come out of the application; I was so accustomed to being disappointed that I accepted defeat before it became a reality.

On my interview date, I got dressed, and guess who took me for my interview? Yep, Jeremy. I think I may have mentioned he was not a great boyfriend, but he cared about me as a person. He was quite kind at the same time that he was mean. He could not commit and was unfaithful, but he never physically abused me, he never told me hurtful things, and he was there for me if I needed anything. If I ever needed to go somewhere, he would take me. Can you blame me for still loving him? He felt that he somehow had to be my guardian, and years after, he would tell me he loved me truly, but he was not built to deal with commitment.

He was my chauffeur for all things important. If I had to go to the bank and had to carry cash, he took me and brought me home. He felt he had to protect me, yet at the same time, he was the one person who hurt me more than anyone else in my life. This can help you to understand my mind and my love. I guess even though we broke up, we still were together on another level, as good friends. No one quite understood that, and people figured we were still together as a couple, but we were not. We could not go back to that stage, or we wouldn't have anything left. I think we both knew that we did not want to lose each other completely.

He waited outside the building whilst I went inside for my interview with the airline, and suddenly I was the star. A photographer was there, took my picture, and said I looked like a good representation of a young woman who wanted to become a professional career woman. I would see my picture in the local newspaper a week after, with a caption: "Young, excited candidate perfect representation of our youth."

I sat in a chair a long time waiting for my turn because it was a group interview, and there were more than one hundred applicants. I was so nervous and excited. Then my name was called, and I went into the boardroom. In the interview, I was sweating profusely in my hands and my feet, and my heart was pounding. I remember some of the questions, but I do not remember my answers. I spoke when I needed to, I shook hands, and that was the end of the interview. I left with my nerves alive, and I felt adrenalin flowing through my veins. I was so excited and thought I really wanted the job, but I was not sure what would happen next.

Jeremy waited for me all this time, and I knew he was there, but I had forgotten about him. This was a life-changing phase, and my mind was on fire. I remember Jeremy dropping me at home and telling me not to be disappointed if I didn't get the job; they usually hired the offspring of the wealthy and people they knew. He did not think I would get the job and thought that I was not flight attendant material. His sister had been a flight attendant for the airline a few years prior.

I listened to Jeremy's words and did not think much about the interview. I went about doing what I was doing before, which was not very much. Then one day, I went home, and my parents gave me a letter from the airline. I had gotten the job! They wanted me to come in and do an orientation and some medical tests, and then I was good to go! There was the start of a new life and perhaps a new person.

I started working at the airline in a few weeks, and life moved really fast after that. I had never even been on an airplane before, and I'd never travelled anywhere but home, work, and a few short distances with my parents. Suddenly I was on an airplane, walking around whilst the plane was in flight, wearing cool clothes (tailored uniforms), and working with really cool people. All the cool people whom I would look at before were working at this airline. They smelt nice, looked nice, and were quite intelligent. The job exposed us to other countries, people, and lifestyles far more than I'd thought. I had read of all these things and never dreamt this would become a reality for me. This was surreal, and the years I spent working as a flight attendant were amazing. I became one of the privileged and envied people of the socially well-known and fancy world. I smelt nice, looked good, and felt on top of the world! I was popular, and guys wanted to date me and would look at me with interest wherever I went. This went to my head and gave me a high that I had never felt before.

I think I attacked this new phase with veracity and a zest to experience as much as I could. I came out of myself. I no longer thought of myself as unattractive. I became someone who could see what she was and wanted more. I felt pretty, even beautiful at times.

I remember my first day, which was awkward but fun. My inexperience showed, and I was just lucky that I had one of my old classmates from high school working with me. She made it much easier for me. Part of the initiation by the older crew was to let newbies mess up and feel bad. I managed to escape the initiation because my friend helped me learn the routine of in-flight service and other flight procedures.

I was introduced as her friend, and she took care of me. She ensured I did not screw up, and when we landed in our first destination, I was like the proverbial fish out of water. Everything was pristine to my eyes, beautiful and unreal. I felt overwhelmed and so was quiet. I usually am quiet if I'm not sure what to say or do. All the buildings seemed too huge and beautiful, the lights were so many, and the stores were so overwhelming. Even the people seemed so impressive in their clothing, and I was lost in my thoughts for a bit. I thought back to when I was younger, and I would read books and daydream about being in some of the worlds created by fiction. Now, here I was living in one such moment! It was so unreal that I wanted someone to pinch me.

I went to the hotel, living in every minute from the deboarding of passengers to coming off the airplane, to getting into the hotel shuttle bus and going to my room. I was all smiles and had endless energy. I was the super worker flight attendant bee!

Good thing for me that I had my friend, who took me around and made me familiar with the hotel, room service, and food places. And good lord, the stores in a local mall! I found that I could not buy anything because I could not believe I was there in person. I wandered around with her and basically reacted automatically; I was consumed by inner thoughts. I am grateful for this period in my life because it offered the opportunity I'd always wanted, which was to grow into my being, like myself, and have the chance to build my personality. I no longer was someone's girlfriend, cast away after being used. I was someone whose future looked bright and big. Here was where I learnt a lot about myself and others, and what really matters in this world: living your life as much as you can, trying to do whatever you do to your best, and not hurting anyone along the way – that's the way we should all act!

I opened my arms and heart to this part of my life, and I loved it. I became quite comfortable with flying and all the experiences associated with my years as a flight attendant. I was truly satisfied with this phase of my life and wanted nothing else.

Along with my new freedom of being away from home, whilst on trips and on layovers, I had the even more welcome freedom of moving away from home! I needed to be living in a certain location for pickup for flights, and my parents did not live within the geographic mappings for the airline. When I told them, my dad was set against it, but I wanted to keep my job, so I suggested a compromise. I didn't move right away. Given what I have told you of my parents, you didn't think it would be easy, did you? But eventually I would move away and live on my own, and my mind would acquire a peace I never knew existed before.

CHAPTER 14

ADVENTURES

I knew that moving away would be hard, so I did not move right away. I left home the day before my flight and carried a change of clothing. I got a temporary place to stay; Patty from my previous job rented a place within my pickup area. I was still in contact with her and asked if I could sublet a room. She was happy because she paid less with me staying there, and now she had company.

Thus began my real growing-up experiences and crazy adventures. I went to each flight and returned to my temporary place, sometimes only needing to spend the night. This was not frowned upon by my parents because it was not a long stay, and I was making really good money, which I generously shared with them. Green makes everyone more at ease with decisions. I knew that they cared about me, but deep down they knew that this was my life to live.

I thought about it, and after a few flights, it became apparent with my frequent comings and goings, I had to make my temporary move more permanent. I figured now would be a great time to introduce a more permanent plan and give me the freedom I craved. I then moved more of my stuff, but not all, because all the space I had at this place was only one room. My older brother helped me, and my father seemed despondent but did not try to stop me.

Between flights, I still went home sometimes if my ground time was more than a day. I appreciated my parents more when I moved. I missed the food and the warmth of family, and sometimes I was lost with all this newfound freedom. It was too much, and sometimes I stayed indoors; even though I could go out as much as I wanted to, I did not want to. I felt scared until I realized this was what I had always wanted. Then I started having adventures!

It seemed to creep up on me unexpectedly. One day I was living with my parents, and the next I was living on my own. Then boom – chaos! I enjoyed staying with Patty, who was quite fun and nice to be around because she was never really serious. She had several boyfriends and was never around; most weekends, she went home to her parents. My time living with Patty was pretty uneventful. I would be alone on weekends but would spend most of my time shopping and going to the library.

The chaos and adventures started when Annie came along. Annie was petite, cute in a strange way, energetic, and fun to be around. She took it upon herself to have me tag along with her everywhere she went – and I mean everywhere. She was very friendly and drew me out of my shell. She was very social, had lots of friends, and liked to go for walks. I was not sure why she liked having me around because as I would later learn from my "friends", I was boring to be around. I was not good with small talk and kept most of my thoughts to myself.

When Patty was not around, I hung out with Annie in between flights. So started the troubled, scary, adventurous part of my life. Until now, all the trouble I'd had was a bad boyfriend experience. Other than that, I was pretty naïve about the ways of the world. I accepted people at face value and never was sceptical. I thought that Annie was who she seemed to be: friendly, nice, and always home. I went with Annie to stores on the street, to the seawalls, and to hang out with her friends. I followed her to meet friends in their workplaces. One strange night, I followed her to a hotel to visit a friend. Granted, I had to wait along with another friend on the street for what seemed like an awful long time, but still nothing registered to me.

What may be apparent to some of you by now was quite lost upon me. It took physical appearances for me to see things for what they were. I also hung out with Annie and her best friend Natasha, who was drop-dead gorgeous and had a somewhat normal-looking boyfriend.

I also hung out with her and a cousin, Chris, who seemed very affectionate with her, always hugging and kissing her. I eventually would get the light bulb moment, and rather rudely too! I remember one weekend when Chris, Annie, and I went to a creek for a swim, and we were goofing about. Annie's cousin was splashing around with her, and suddenly she screamed and started looking around frantically. Have I mentioned my extreme fear of snakes? I was so scared that I almost jumped out of my skin, my heart threatening to pop out of my mouth. In my frozen state, I heard Annie repeatedly screaming, "My teeth, my teeth!"

Then I saw a gaping hole at the front of her mouth. It seemed that Annie wore dentures, and they had fallen into the creek. Her cousin hugged and consoled her, and then we returned home. I was now thinking of my new place as home. When we got home, Annie was even more inconsolable. She said she looked so ugly with no teeth. The fact is she did look a little older, but she was not quite ugly, just a little weird. I wanted to laugh at the same time I wanted to tell her it was okay, so I kept quiet.

Then it started. The following week, I arrived from a flight and went to collect my pay. I came home and was checking my pay. Annie saw me and said, "Wow, that's a lot of money." I did not think much of the statement; Annie never went to work, but she always seemed to have money. I put it away, and later that day, I left to visit my parents. I came back a few days later. Annie was waiting for me, or it seemed that way. The vibes were emanating and spooked me, but only a little. I started seeing a little bit more of her intense side. By this time, Patty had moved out. She moved right out of the country and got married to someone, not one of her boyfriends, and that was that. I never gave another thought to her because I was preoccupied with Annie, who had fully asserted herself into my free time.

Annie now stayed in Patty's room, which contained the only bathroom and toilet. I was uncomfortable with the fact that every time I needed to shower and use the toilet, I had to enter Annie's room. I could not avoid Annie even if I tried. After Patty moved, it seemed that Annie made me her centre of everything. I wanted to fly every day now, and when I was home for longer than a few hours, I wanted to go home to my parents but lacked the courage to say no to Annie.

We ate dinner together, and when I came back from flights, no matter how late it was, she was up waiting for me. Time passed after that incident where Annie had lost her teeth, and it was a few weeks after she had made reference to my money. One day she turned to me and started crying. I asked why, and she said she did not have the money to replace her teeth. She asked if she could borrow from me. I am quite generous and also a big sucker for those who appear less fortunate. I could not bring myself to lend her the money, so I gave her half of what the cost was for her teeth replacement, and she was grateful. I knew I was a sucker, but what could I do? She was crying and was so pitiful!

Then came dinners. She had no money for dinner or for groceries. I thought it would be easier to share. Even now, I am too generous, and maybe that's why I am not very rich. I am still learning how to not give away and not be a sucker. I wondered how my money went so fast, and I could not hold on to it for long because I was pulled into the pitiful stories. First the teeth, then the groceries, then other issues: eyes, doctor bill, and a john coming to collect money!

Yes, you heard me right: john as in a pimp. And so came to light her true nature: she was a whore. That being said, it still did not penetrate my stupid head, but I started feeling out of sorts. It came to an end for me one night after my flight. I came home really late, and I needed to go to the washroom. Remember where it was located? I had to pass through Annie's room to get to it. It was late, and I didn't want to disturb her, so I silently crept. Maybe I should have marched in with bells. Lo and behold, there was Annie and her best friend Natasha, naked as baboons and splashed over each other!

I still cringe at the memory, thought I don't remember much. I think my mind failed me, and I drew a blank. I remember Annie and Natasha rushing around, grabbing clothes, and giving weak and weird explanations. I knew what I had to do and did it expeditiously. Within a week, I was out of there! This is a moment I've tried forgetting, but it lives on. I remembered thinking, *And I thought I was all grown up! Life has so much more to give, and I should go get it!*

Chapter 15

Next New Place

The next place I moved into was huge and seemed really nice and sunny. There was lots of cleaning to do because it had been vacant for quite some time, and the owner had let it sit there. I did lots of dusting, scrubbing, and scraping, but afterwards it looked homely and nice. Then came the night – oh, my! It became a spooky hotel, filled with dust and nightmarish shadows. It was too huge for little old me. The place I rented was the entire third floor of a house, and the stairs, which were outside of the building, were rickety but cute. I stayed there for one night and had a flight the next day. I got no sleep but thought nothing of it. The place was new to me, and I figured I would soon get accustomed to it.

When I got picked up by the crew bus, the entire crew was appalled that I was staying in this neighbourhood, in a huge house on the third floor by myself! Caryll was a flight attendant who seemed genuinely more concerned than the others; I didn't know quite how much until after a few days. When we returned from the flight, she was aghast that I was staying all alone in the huge house, and it was really late when the bus dropped me off.

She mentioned that the neighbourhood was really terrible, and there were a lot of burglaries and drug addicts.

I didn't think much of it, other than the fact that I never quite slept whilst renting this place. I then had a few days at home between flights, and I became scared shitless and thought about how I had paid for three months in advance. I was young, had a good amount of disposable cash, and was entirely world stupid! I figured I was safe and Caryll was being overly concerned.

Caryll called me during my days off after this flight and asked me to come by her house. I got dressed and went over – anything to not be home alone. Then she took me to her neighbour across the street, who was a wonderful, warm human being. I will tell you more about Mrs Marvin a little later.

Mrs Marvin looked me over and said, "Well, young lady, I heard that you are looking for somewhere to live and have nowhere to go." Caryll had told her a rather touching story and told me to play along. I did, and the very next week, I moved into this lovely place, where I felt at home for a few years. Mrs Marvin would become my closest person next to my mom.

I notified my current landlady, and boy, did she give me a hard time. She insisted that I fork over the entire three months' rent, even though there was no written contract. My stupidity had no boundaries, and I quietly handed it over to avoid a conflict. In retrospect, I have been robbed by quite a few individuals. There was this flight attendant that borrowed money from me, and she never gave it back even when I asked. I seem to have a knack for giving away things: money, pride – the list goes on.

Anyhow, I moved into this wonderful home where I was welcomed from the very first day as if I was family. I still remember Mrs Marvin's face when I moved in and came home after the first flight with goodies for her. She was so happy and surprised. She started inviting me up for dinner (I lived on the lower floor), but I was a person who always ran away from too much familiarity and needed my personal space. I loved my new home, and so did my dad, who came to visit. Now that I think of it, my mother never visited me at any of the places I rented. I never asked her to; I guess it was because I still saw her. Between my flights and my ground time, I often went home and spent the entire day relaxing with my parents. I think my mom felt too strange visiting me; in her mind, she kept a picture of her little girl still at home. She most likely felt sad and out of place visiting me, so she felt that it was better to have me come home to her.

At home, I had home-cooked meals and could just be. I wanted all my life to get away from my family, and now that I was away, I wanted to be with them. This is so typical of us. We want what we cannot have, and when we have it, it does not align with our expectations, or the challenge is lost, and somehow it doesn't seem as appealing as before.

I always wanted my mom to be happy. I don't know how she did things with no one seeing her pain and sadness each day. I did, but as a young person, sometimes I forgot and was mean and callous. I think I was too self-centred and thought that I was better than my parents. I became fussy, and I think I am still a bit of a fussy individual. I like things to make sense, I like seemingly perfect people, I like clean things, and the list goes on. If something seems not to fit and does not fall neatly into the picture, I am upset. Maybe that's why I could not keep any relationship for a long time. Then again, maybe I was being too hard on myself; after all, I did go out with Jeremy for a long time – too many years.

I lived in the new place I thought of as home for almost two years. The landlady and her family were so nice to me. I worked as a flight attendant during that time. I think time really does fly when you are busy. I spent most of the months away from home and in different countries. I also spent a lot of my time home with my parents, and then I started hanging out with other flight attendants.

Along came the parties, drinking, and having good times with my friends. We still did not cross boundaries; we did not do drugs or sleep around, even though everyone thought we did. In contrary to my usual habits of overanalyzing everything and thinking before drinking, spending, and hanging out, I changed. I spent all my money on going out, and then the rest went to my parents, who I knew needed money. I spent money on rent, a little on buying stuff for myself, some on socializing, and the rest to support my parents and brothers.

While partying with my friends, time flew by, catching me up in the whirlwind and making my head spin. I knew this could not continue, and I also knew most of this was due to no freedom earlier, heartbreak, and a lack of confidence. Actions without thoughts were common. Also, I wanted to live a life free of Jeremy, and I felt that filling it up with friends, parties, family, and work would ease the pain.

I knew that one of my main reasons for not being logical was keeping my ex-boyfriend in my life. If he was there, he still was part of my life and of what I felt and did. I wanted to break away, and I tried, but every time I was down in the dumps, who turned up but my ex.

I wanted to live my life and have the experiences everyone else had. I wanted to be happy, and I had it for the next few years.

Chapter 16

Life with Mark

Meet Mark: charmingly handsome and sexy as hell. He smiled across the room in the bar, and I glanced at him from the stool where I sat. I saw him bend his head and whisper something to one of his friends, who came over to us.

I felt a little strange because I had not dated anyone after Jeremy, and I did not have any experience with other guys. I turned my back and waited, hoping that his friend would chat with my friends and that I was mistaken. I was attracted but not keen on starting a relationship or dating anyone. He tapped me on the shoulder and looked me in the eyes, shrugging to indicate Mark, who was busy looking anywhere else but at me. His friend's name was Tim, and he had come over to tell me that Mark was interested in me but was too shy to come over.

I was weirdly out of balance and did not want to act on this. I smiled and did not say anything. Shortly after the little chat, my friends and I left to go dancing at a club. We had a blast and partied into the early hours of the morning. I forgot all about Mark and this little encounter.

I left to go to a flight the next day, and after that I had a few more flights. That night flew out of my mind until my friend Dawn, whom I was having lunch with that day, leaned over and asked me if I remembered Mark. I said, "Yes, he was that cute guy in the bar a few months ago." She said he had asked her boyfriend for my telephone number and wanted to get together. That threw me in a tizzy because I never had to plan and think about a relationship. As a matter of fact, I had no experience in starting a relationship because it had just happened with Jeremy. Also, I'd known Jeremy from school, whereas I knew nothing about Mark.

I shook my head and said to Dawn, "I am not sure about this." I wanted to date Mark, but I was scared. I still thought I had all these flaws waving in the air around me, and I felt insecure when it came to thinking about going out with another guy. She insisted that I try a date with Mark, and after a prolonged discussion of pros and cons, I said yes.

Mark called me, and we chatted. I was sweating buckets on the other end of the line because I did not know much about chatting and flirting with guys. I listened more than I spoke, and Mark wanted to take me out. Mark came for me that same night to take me out to dinner. My palms were so wet with sweat that I hoped he wouldn't touch me. I felt so stupid and socially awkward. What did I say and do? He looked at me, and he had the sweetest smile ever. He said to me, "Are you nervous?" I said yes. He took my hands, which were still wet, and dried them on his shirt. He then leaned over and kissed me ever so softly on the lips. I did not know what to do. This was all new to me.

I imagine the rest of the night went well, because the rest blurred by. I became so entranced that I kept staring at Mark's face and lips. I melted at the end of the night. I was not accustomed to romance, and he oozed of it. Then, before

I knew it, he was dropping me home, and he placed another kiss on my lips, which was a little more heated this time. My blood was humming, and my heart was doing a little dip as I walked into my apartment. I could not believe the feeling. So this was what those romance novels were talking about! I did not have this feeling with Jeremy, and it was all new. I slept soundly because I was so exhausted from the tension of being on a date. Imagine me, on a date after Jeremy. Well, look at me now, people – someone still wanted me! I know I seemed needy, but when you remember what I went through, you will realize that it demolishes you for a major part of your life, unless you have a network that supports you and builds you back up.

I awoke with a smile on my face, and as soon as I had breakfast, I showered and then read a book. I was in between flights and had a few days of ground time. I wanted to calm my nerves and did not know what to expect the day after a date. I was so surprised when the phone rang around 10 a.m. It was Mark, and he wanted to know if we could go on another date. I said yes and then got really giddy.

I hung up and started smiling to myself, checking my outfits. I wasn't sure where we were going, so I decided on jeans and a T-shirt. I dressed quite simply and did not like a lot of make-up. I liked clean lines and plain solid colours, and most of all, I liked to feel comfortable in my clothes. My friends would make fun of me when they went shopping with me. If I saw a pair of shoes I liked (coloured brown or black), I would buy a few pairs. I guess I was a bit boring in my fashion style.

Now, let us go back to my exciting plans for my date. I busied myself all day long, cleaning and fussing and trying to make the day go by faster. Mark was going to pick me up for dinner. Just when I thought the day was lingering, it was time for my second date. I got flustered and panicky, wondering where this would lead to and what to do. I felt like I was about to explode from excitement.

Mark was very charming. He had this dimple when he smiled, and I noticed it the first night I saw him. I knew from the fluttering in my heart that he may be trouble. He was very rich, handsome, and popular. He had an appeal that made him dangerous yet enticing, and I wanted to know more and feel more.

The doorbell rang, and I went to the door (I lie – I was waiting behind the door, and I counted a few seconds) and opened it. There was Mark with a bouquet of flowers and the sweetest smile. I stood there quite sure I was smiling foolishly, and then I took the flowers and thanked him with a peck on the cheek. I went into the kitchen, grabbed a glass, filled it with water, and placed the flowers in it. I then turned to leave, but Mark was right behind me. As I turned, my face was a few inches away from his. He grabbed my chin, turned my lips to his, and kissed me. My blood rushed somewhere, and I was tingling from every nerve. This was unbelievable that I could feel this nervous and excited around someone else other than Jeremy. I felt squishy inside, and my brains went to mush.

Mark took my hand, and we went to dinner. I tried eating; somehow the kiss had made my mind race and my stomach queasy. I played with my food and tried to engage in conversation. In my mind, I kept thinking, *What happens next? How do I know if we are meeting again?* Imagine being in a relationship for quite a few years, and not knowing anything other than it makes you quite ignorant of the dating world's rules and expectations. I was clueless.

After dinner, we went for a drive to a park, where we sat and chatted; there was a lot to talk about. I found Mark to be quite intelligent, and he had a great sense of humour. He had lived and studied in another country for four years, and he told me about some of his growing experiences, which were a little horrifying. He went to university in the Bronx, and there were gangs at his school that picked on him and beat him up quite often. He told me of one incident where they kicked him over and over, and he curled up into a ball so his stomach won't get hurt. That was when his parents decided to bring him back home, so he could be safe and happy.

My relationship with Mark was stormy, fast, unpredictable, and full of passion. I loved every moment of it. He was full of energy, attentive, sexy as hell, charming, and great to hang out with. I went out with him every day I was at home that week, and then I started my flight roster for the month. We did not get serious in that week; it was all fun and hanging out, with a few kisses here and there. I wanted to go slow, but at the same time, I wanted to go fast. He was so charming and such a great kisser; he made me feel alive all over!

Within a month we were sleeping together and could not get enough of each other. We were so good together, and I felt true passion. I felt grown up and no longer a girl, but a woman. I took control in bed and wanted more and more. I became insatiable around Mark, and he seemed the same with me. Sometimes after a flight, he would be there waiting for me in my apartment (I gave him a key after a few months). We would not leave to go out for the few days when I was on the ground.

I started hanging out with Mark and his friends. They were a really cool group of people, and they consisted of all the popular girls and boys of the city. We went to a lot of parties and dinners. I learnt in the first month with Mark that he was a racer and had a wild side. I liked that about him; it made him more alluring, and I felt happy when I was with him.

I went to my first car race at the local race course. It was packed, and I got a front seat to see my wonderful boyfriend race. He was good and fast! I found everything about him so daring and exciting. I didn't want this to end, yet I had no future plans, unlike when I was with Jeremy, where I wanted to live with him forever. I did find myself falling in love with Mark. We spent so much time together, the passion was real, and I was so happy with him. I did not think of a future because it was too heady, and I simply wanted to live in the moment.

I forgot to tell you that he was two years younger than me. This did not make any difference except for the fact that at that age, young men get scared when they are in a relationship for too long. It makes the word "commitment" seem much more real and like an impending sentence.

I fell into a routine. Whenever I was between flights, I spent all my time with Mark. I did not even go by my parents as much – only occasionally to drop off money and stay for an hour or two. I got caught in the same trap of loving someone more than myself and giving it my all. There was no time for me, no time to think things through, and I started to suffocate. I imagine that's how Mark must have started to feel. He was too alive and vibrant to want to be with someone all the time. He seemed to start getting a little angry over little things, and he became a little cold. He pulled away and would be disconnected when we went out with his friends. He seemed to want to chat more with his friends than he did with me, and I noticed he would glance furtively at other girls.

I remember coming home from one flight in the first few months of our relationship, before things started getting sour. I found cute little stuffed animals with hearts all over my apartment. When I counted them, there were more than fifty! Mark had placed these in every single spot he thought I would visit during my return home. That was when I fell in love with him; it was the sweetest, most romantic moment in my life. I know that not all relationships last, so I will say at this moment that before things started going sour, Mark seemed so real, and I felt as if we were soul mates with a deep connection. He made me understand what romance was. He cared for me and was such a macho guy that it made it more endearing. He would tell me to not ever disclose to his friends the way he was with me, because they would poke fun at him.

I remember being sick one day, and Mark rushed to get me food and medicine that he thought would help me feel better. He rented movies, and we rested and looked at movies all day. I started to feel that I could not be without him and wanted a forever with him. It's funny how, even though I wanted these things, I started suffocating around the same time he did. We never talked about it, and it ended rather messily. I know that on the first day I went out with him, we would never end up together forever, but I still wanted to have that time with him, and I am happy I took that chance and spent the time.

I remember when it all came to a stop. The romance ended, and along came the bitterness and sadness. Mark and I went to a soca festival, and all the popular people were there. Mark and I danced our hearts away. That was another thing he did to me: he broke down my inhibitions, and I felt free to do whatever I wanted around him, which was why sex with him was so great! Then I felt him stiffening slightly and drawing away. I looked into his face and saw him looking into the distance. He was staring at a beautiful girl in a rather skimpy dress. She was staring right back at him. There was no more dancing; the mood had changed. Mark said he was tired and would like to go home. My heart stopped; here was the moment of truth. I knew in my soul that this was the end. I did not show any reaction and waited for it to come to a boil.

I don't think I said anything at all. My intuition usually is spot-on, and I knew what was looming in the near future. There was no turning back from this. My heart was crumbling harshly in my body, I felt physical pain stabbing my insides, and tears were threatening. By the time Mark dropped me home, I was a sobbing mess, and he apparently could not deal with that. He very meanly told me to stop, and he left me standing at my door. I fell to the ground. I know you see this in movies and think its overkill, but when you are truly in love with someone, it crushes you and makes all else seem irrelevant. I stayed on the floor for hours, crying and wailing like I had lost someone for good, which I had. It was such a dark, sad place to be. I remember thinking in the midst of my tears, *This is so dramatic. Why are you doing this?* But I could not stop myself from falling apart.

I cried myself to sleep after I dragged myself to bed. I slept in all day, and the days flew by. Then I went to work. Flight after flight, I cheerfully smiled at the passengers, overworking myself. For flights no one wanted, I volunteered. The more time I was away from home and busy, the better I felt. I spent more time out of the country than in it and started to feel a bit better. I did not go out because that would have been social suicide – seeing Mark with the girl he had been staring at, him happily wrapped in her arms. I was so despondent when I was home that my friends started intervening. I fought back and refused to answer the phone. I did not go to the door when they came and was rude when I did speak to them. I pushed them away so I could drown in my misery and self-loathing.

My friends had stayed away when I was with Mark; they'd never liked him because they knew the side of him I saw after we broke up. He was a player, he was sexy, and he was handsome and charming, but he never stayed in a relationship for long. He constantly broke young girls' hearts. My friends had tried warning me about him during our relationship, and instead of listening, I had shunned them. I did what most of us do: I thought they were jealous and knew nothing about what we had. I still do not regret the time I spent with him, and I do not dislike him to this day. We had something special, but then it wore out. We had great sex and a unique connection, but we both were not ready for a serious relationship. At that time, I did not want it to end. I was too much in love, and being in love and falling out of love hurts badly and keeps logic from being part of the equation.

My friends tried setting me up with blind dates, but I refused to go out. It didn't matter who it was and what he looked like; I did not want to see anyone else after Mark. He had made me feel alive, and now I felt dead. I felt that I needed to be by myself for a while.

CHAPTER 17

ILLUSIONS OF A BETTER LIFE

For months I was such a drag to be around that my friends started to avoid me and not call me anymore. They had tried stopping by and spending time with me. I started going by my parents' home more and more, and they seemed to pick up that something was wrong. I did not tell them because my parents had been crushed and demoralised with my relationship with Jeremy. That was enough for them. I would manage my own pains. I did not want to share any more misery with them; they had been through enough. I kept everything to myself and dealt with it.

I spent months doing things for myself, and I became religious. One of my friends managed to drag with her to visit some of her friends, a young couple with a baby who was so adorable. My heart broke a little when I saw the baby, as it did every time I came near one. I never forgot what I'd done during my relationship with Jeremy; even now, it is hard to say the word. Every time I saw a baby, I always did a quick math calculation in my mind to see how old my children would be, and I also kept the dates in my mind. They were such nice people, and they made me smile at how much they loved their baby and each other. My friend Amber told me these were her friends from the church she went to, and if I liked, I could go along with her next Sunday.

I thought about it. I did not have any plans and had no flights, so I said yes. This was my reintroduction into the world of religion, and I sought and found refuge. Everyone was warm and welcoming and made me feel part of the congregation. I started going every Sunday I was at home, and I also attended the youth sessions. These were fun because they showed movies (religious but still fun to watch), and it was great hanging out with no romance, no complications, just clean fun with a group of young people who were simple and nice. I felt somehow that this made me at peace with all the pain I had experienced in my life, and after a few months, realized that I could have a better life; I could do more. All I had to do was start dreaming again, and put my dreams to realization. I was strong and older now; I knew what I wanted and liked myself. There would be no stopping me.

The youth group consisted of some elders who were the same age as me, and they were so much fun. We hung out a lot and walked home together, and sometimes they came by my apartment to chat. There was one person in the group whom I had met a few times before but had never really spoken to. It was strange how I met this person again, and of all places, it was at a church.

I remember the time I met this person. When I was training to become a flight attendant, there was a huge, intimidating swimming pool we had to conquer – correction, I had to conquer. I was deathly afraid of the water and drowning, and it took me a long time to overcome that fear. During one of my swimming lessons, I saw this quiet and handsome guy walking by. My friend Marcy, whom I was with, dared me to say hello. She had this weird habit of daring me to do things, and I would without hesitation. Man, the things I have done on a dare with Marcy!

Anyhow, I followed through on the dare. I went to the guy and said hello. I felt braver with no fear. It was so funny and cute, the way he stopped and dropped to my level; I was in the pool, and he was walking by. He said hi and extended his hand, which I shook. Then I put my head into the pool and swam away. When I returned, he had left. I never got his name and forgot all about it.

A few weeks later I saw him in a grocery store, where I again said hi quickly. Then I went to another aisle, paid hastily, and left. I felt embarrassed when I saw him again because I thought considering I had never seen him before, it would be a rare chance of encountering him again.

This guy, Dean, was in the youth group at the church. We became friends, and he came by quite often to hang out with the group by my apartment. He started coming by to visit me alone, and we would listen to music, watch movies, and chat for hours. Nothing came out of it; he was too genteel and polite to make a move, and I was too jaded. He was very attractive and intelligent, and he was an aspiring artist (and from what I saw, quite talented). I was still reeling from my relationships and wanted to feel safe. I know that I had suffered when Mark had left me, but like I said, I had no regrets. Being with Jeremy had made me feel complete, and without him, the void never seemed to be filled. My experience with Jeremy had scarred me much more than being with Mark; I had given my soul to Jeremy.

Dean seemed interested in me, but I got mixed signals and refused to be hurt again or hurt someone else, so I never took the initiative, and neither did he. Dean and I spent a lot of time together, we went to church, I went home to visit a few times, and we became inseparable. We went for long walks and hung out at parties.

I think this was when I started believing in myself, and I spent more time with friends. I did not date for a long period, which helped me discover myself and realize what potential I had. I also began to have a lighter feeling, a sense of peace, which I attributed to regularly attending church. It was a combination of not needing someone else, finding my value, and spending time with positive people. I started believing there was a better life for me – not one spent chasing a guy, spending my money casually, and having my mind and heart torn apart. I did not date Dean because this never occurred to me; I figured he was a good friend and wanted no more than that, and he never crossed the line. I also did not feel good about myself; I felt used, washed up, and not good enough for anyone. With church and Dean and all things positive in my life, I became myself and lived each day doing things that made me happy, not living vicariously through a boyfriend. Dean never made a move because Jeremy persisted in being present in my life. I did not know how that affected anyone else trying to be in my life until later. Dean felt that he did not stand a chance against Jeremy.

Thus starts another phase in my life. My life became calmer, and I saw things differently. People did not irk me so easily, and my finances were in order. Everything seemed to be going so well.

I did not know why I thought life was hard and everything seemed against me. For those who like to go to church and follow a religious path, kudos for you. For those who don't and yet find the same peace and tranquillity others may not find without guidance and belief, I also respect that.

We are all different, and yet we are all susceptible to errors and feelings. I think having Dean in my life at this stage helped me immensely. I started to see that life had been difficult because I allowed it to be, and I did not take control of my life when I should have. We can all stop the madness, hurt, and pain if we are strong and wise. Unfortunately, it's easier said than done.

Chapter 18

Doors Opening and Closing

The air was fresh and brisk as I walked along the sidewalks with the sun warming my face. Thoughts were flowing through my mind: go to the hairdresser, then go get groceries, and then visit my parents. Walking in the sunshine, with the breeze rustling the trees overhead and people passing by, made me happy. I felt happy and wanted to feel that way forever. I did not have to worry about someone else and feel hurt or scared. It was great to feel light and alive. I was at peace.

I went to the hairdresser, and she was such a cheerful and energetic person. She loved to gossip, but it was done as something to pass the time with clients. She chatted so much that time would fly by, and I would spend the entire day at the salon without knowing where the hours went!

I sat in the chair and reflected. In the mirror was someone who was still rather pretty, young, and full of life. There was no washed-up girl or broken doll looking back at me. It was all the internal suffering that made me feel it showed outside. My heart felt full, and my mind was racing towards the possibilities I now saw in my life. I knew that there was so much more to life. I had spent so many years living my life for others, being consumed with feelings, and seeing things through a lens marred by narrow vision. I now saw that the world was huge and exciting, and it was all mine to explore and see. I felt excited because this was my time to explore all the endless possibilities, and I felt that I could do anything and no one could stop me. This inspired me to think about my next phase in life, and I started thinking ahead and wanting more.

I visited my parents and was so hyped that nothing they said made me feel down. I loved my parents and also enjoyed going home; it made me feel like a child and protected. However, the visits could get quite tiresome and depressing when they started nagging. Not even the repeated sentences of how I was getting old and not married brought me down that day. I heard the words, but the impact was not hurtful; rather, it resonated with me and provided fuel for my inspirations, newfound freedom, and realizations. I knew then that I had to travel even more and find out more about myself.

I decided to book several trips and went with a few friends to different places. My friend Tracey, who was fun to hang out with, was pretty and looked a bit like me. Everywhere we went, people thought we were sisters. We went to Barbados, and then I went to Curacao and Montreal with another friend. It was awesome, and I wondered why I'd thought being in a relationship was the natural path when there was so much more in life that did not require me to have a boyfriend or partner.

I enjoyed visiting Barbados, driving along those narrow and mad roads with even crazier fast drivers. I'd go all the way up the hill and look down. When driving up, it provided an illusion of being under the sea whilst still on the hill, the curves looping to provide that surreal feeling and optical trick. It is an experience I cannot fully describe; you have to experience it yourself. I loved the air, the people, and the places in Barbados. I liked going to the clubs and standing on the decks, with the water lapping against the poles. The clubs were situated on the beach, and the decks were strategically placed over the sea, so it felt as if the entire club was in the sea. The nightlife was so cheerful, and there was live music with great food. During the day, we took taxis downtown to visit the tourist spots and hang out in the markets. We stayed for a week and enjoyed ourselves a lot.

I went to Curacao with Andrea, who was smaller than me in size, bolder, and younger. When we hung out, we would have so much fun together. The weather in Curacao is extremely hot, and there are no trees and large buildings to provide shelter. Most of the island is fully exposed to the sun! I became charred, but it was so beautiful. The architecture was old and colourful, and everything seemed so romantic. There were cobblestoned roads, and the waterfront was such a sight. It was the perfect place for young people to visit. The people were friendly, and the clubs were better than those in Barbados. There was salsa, and everyone seemed to be into the dancing. There were quite a few clubs to choose from for a small island.

On our first day, we went to the famous aquarium, where we spent all day. Then we went to the beaches. The aquarium was massive and interesting; we saw sea life that we didn't know existed. We stayed for a few more days and then returned home to go back to work.

Later on that year, Andrea and I went to Montreal. It was my first time going to Montreal, and I knew it would be cold, so we made sure we had our warm gear ready. The churches were impressive, old, and filled with character. We stayed at Andrea's uncle's house, and he had two little boys. We were supposed to sleep in the boys' room, but Andrea had the bright idea for us to sleep in the basement on top of beanbags. Please don't ever try this. When you wake, body parts you never knew you had will hurt all day long!

We went to a few flea markets. Maybe it's not the best of adventures for some people, but for us, it was. We went and felt that we got some great deals. I came away with so many clothes in good condition, so I was happy. It was a fun time in my life, and I felt good. I was a bit regretful that I had spent so many years not living my life and instead getting kicked around. I was over being in a relationship. (I lament too much. I know.)

I was having so much fun just being myself and not living vicariously through anyone else. I felt free! I started wondering what I should do with my life. What should I do, and what should I become?

I looked through the window, and the world seemed big. The world was my oyster, so I embarked upon my journey. Thus starts the next era of my journey into life, afresh with good thoughts, confidence, and awareness.

At this time in my life, things have changed. I want you to know that given the path I have taken, I can now do whatever I truly want, and not just think or say I can. I am now living in a different country, surrounded by people and opportunities that will make me grow into a successful person. I am also happy with my life … but that's another story to be told sometime in the future.

Printed in the United States
By Bookmasters